ELEMENT 79

ELEMENT 79

BY FRED HOYLE

NAL

THE NEW AMERICAN LIBRARY

*Published by The New American Library, Inc.
1301 Avenue of the Americas,
New York, New York 10019*

Published simultaneously in Canada by
General Publishing Company, Ltd.

Printed in the United States of America

CONTENTS

ELEMENT
79

ZOOMEN

In the second half of July I was able to get away on a two-week vacation. I decided to go off "Munro-bagging" in the Scottish Highlands. Hotel accommodation being difficult in the Highlands in the summer, especially for a single person, I hired a caravan with a car to match. Driving north the first day, I got precisely to the Scottish border immediately south of Jedburgh. The evening was beautifully fine. I argued I didn't want to spend the whole of the morrow driving, if indeed the morrow was going to be as clear as this. The obvious tactic was to be away at the first light of dawn. By ten o'clock I could be well across the Lowlands. Then I could spend the afternoon "doing" one of the southern peaks, perhaps in the Ben Lawers range.

It fell out as I had planned. I reached Killin not much after ten A.M., found a caravan site, bought fresh meat and other provisions in the town, and set off for Glen Lyon, with the intention of walking up Meall Ghaordie. The afternoon was as fine and beautiful as it could possibly be. I quitted the car at the nearest point to my mountain and set off across the lower bogland. I moved upward at a deliberately slow pace, in part because this was my first day on the hills, in part because the sun was hot. I remember the myriads of tiny colored flowers under my feet. It took about two hours to the summit. I sat down there and munched a couple of apples. Then I laid myself flat on a grassy knoll, using my rucksack for a pillow. The early start and the warm day together had made me distinctly sleepy. It was not more than a minute, I suppose, before I nodded off.

I have fallen asleep quite a number of times on a mountain top. The wakening always produces a slight shock, presumably because you are heavily conditioned to waking indoors. There is always a perceptible moment during which you hunt for your bearings. It was so on this occasion, except the shock was deeper. There was a first moment when I expected to be in a normal bedroom, then a moment in which I remembered that by rights I should be on the summit of a mountain, then a moment when I had become aware of the place where I had in fact awakened and knew it was not at all the right place, not the summit of Meall Ghaordie.

The room I was in was a large rectangular box. I scrambled to my feet and started to inspect the place. Perhaps it may seem absurd to imply that a boxlike room needed inspection, particularly when it was quite empty. Yet there were two very queer things about it. The light was artificial, for the box was wholly opaque and closed, except where a passageway opened out of one of the walls. The distribution of the light was strange. For the life of me I simply could not determine where it was coming from. There were no obvious bulbs or tubes. It almost seemed as if the walls themselves were aglow. They were composed of some material which looked to my inexpert eye merely like one of the many new forms of plastic. But in that case how could light be coming out of such a material?

The box was not nearly as large as I had at first thought. The dimensions in fact were roughly thirty by fifty feet, the height about twenty feet. The lighting produced the impression of a place the size of a cathedral, an effect I have noticed before in underground caves.

The second strange thing was my sense of balance. Not that I found it difficult to stand or anything crude like that. When climbing a mountain the legs quickly become sensitive to balance. If I had not just come off a mountain, it is likely the difference would have passed unnoticed. Yet I could feel a difference of some kind, slight but definite.

My explorations naturally led to the passageway, which didn't go straight for very far. Round a bend I came to a forking point. I paused to remember the division. There were more twists and turns, so that soon I had the strong impression of being in a maze. It gave me the usual moment of panic, of feeling I had lost my way. Then I reflected I had no "way" to lose. Instantly I became calm again and simply strolled where my fancy dictated. The passage eventually brought me back to the large boxlike room. There in the middle of it was my rucksack, the rucksack against which I had laid my head on the summit of Meall Ghaordie. I tried several times and always I came back to the boxlike room. Although the passages had the semblance of a multitude of branches, this also was an illusion. In fact there were eight distinct ways through the system. I managed to get the time required for a single "transit" of the passageways down to about ninety seconds, so the whole arrangement, if not actually poky, was not very large in size. It was just that it was made to seem large.

I did still another turn through the passageways and was startled on this occasion to hear running feet ahead of me. My heart thumped madly, for although I might have seemed calm outwardly, fear was never very far from my side. Around the corner ahead burst a girl of about eighteen or so clad in a dressing gown. At the sight of me, standing there blocking the passageway, she let out a nerve-shattering scream. She stood for twenty or thirty seconds and then flung herself with extreme violence into my arms. "Where are we?" she sobbed, "where are we?" She went on repeating her question, clutching me with a good, powerful muscular grip. Without in any way exceeding natural propriety, I held her closely; it was a natural enough thing to do in the circumstances. Suddenly I felt an acute nausea sweep through me, akin to the late stages of seasickness. The clinch between us dissolved in a flash, for the girl must have felt the same sickness, since she instantly burst out with a violent fit of vomiting.

We both stood there panting. I steadied myself against the wall of the passageway for my knees felt weak. "And who might you be?"

"Giselda Horne," she answered. The voice was American.

"You'd better take that thing off," I said, indicating the dressing gown, now the worse for wear from the sickness.

"I suppose so. I was in a room down here when I came to." The girl led the way to a box, precisely square as far as I could tell, opening out of the very passageway. I felt certain I must have passed this spot many times, but there had been no opening before. Giselda Horne staggered into the box, moaning slightly. I made to follow but soon stopped. I was only just inside when another wave of sickness hit me in the pit of the stomach. Some instinct prompted me to step back into the passage. As I did so, silently and rapidly a panel slid back closing off the box. With the double attack I was hard put to it to take any action, but I did manage to shout through to the girl and to bang my fist on the panel. If she made any answer I was unable to hear it. I tried to walk off the sickness by touring through and through the system of passages, but to no avail. I felt just as rotten as before. At quite some length, for I must have gone through the system many times by other routes before I found it, I came on exactly such a square box as Giselda Horne had gone into. With some apprehension I stepped inside it. Two things happened. A similar panel slid closed behind me, and within thirty seconds the sickness had gone.

This box was a cube with sides about twelve feet. It contained absolutely nothing except a heavy metal door, let into one of the walls, which opened to a moderate tug. Inside was a volume about the size of a fairish oven, in which I found a platter covered with stuff. Before I could examine it further the nausea started again. This time it seemed as if I too would reach the vomiting stage. Just in time the panel slid open and I staggered into the passage with the irrational thought that I must reach the toilet before my stomach hit the roof. Out in the passage the sickness dropped steeply away. In minutes I felt quite normal again. Then suddenly it started up once more, the paneling opened, as if to invite me back into the box, and once inside the sickness was gone. The process was repeated thrice more, in and out of the box. Long before the end of the lesson I knew exactly what it meant–move in, move out, to orders. From where? I had no idea, but one thing the lesson had done for me, my fears had quite gone. Manifestly I was under some kind of surveillance, a surveillance whose mode of operation I couldn't remotely guess. Yet instead of my fears being increased, the exact opposite happened. From this point on, I was not only outwardly calm but I was inwardly master of myself.

With the passing of the sickness I felt quite hungry. Apart from a light lunch on the slopes of Meall Ghaordie, my last meal had been at five A.M. on the Scottish border. I tried the stuff on the platter in the oven. It was neither pleasant nor unpleasant, about like vegetable marrow. How nutritive it was I couldn't tell at all, so I simply ate until I was no longer hungry.

Next I noticed the floor was softer here than it was in the passage or than it was in the big rectangular box. It would be quite tolerable to sleep on. It was harder than the usual bed, but after the first two or three days it would seem comfortable enough. What about a toilet? There was nothing here in the box at all appropriate to a toilet. So how did one fare if taken short with the panel closed? I determined to put the matter to test. I made preparations to use the floor of the box itself. I didn't get very far, nor had I expected to do. The sickness came, the panel slid by, and within a minute I found a new box opening out off the passage. Stepping inside I discovered one large and one small compartment. The small compartment was obviously the privy, for it had a hole about a foot in diameter in its floor. I made the best use of it I could, wondering what I should do for toilet paper. My thoughts on this somewhat embarrassing subject were interrupted by a veritable deluge descending on my head from above. I hopped out of the smaller compartment into the large one. Here the downpour was somewhat less intense, about the intensity of a good powerful shower. Within seconds I was soaked to the skin. The shower stopped and I began to peel off my sodden clothes. I had just about stripped when the shower started up again. Evidently it went off periodically, every three or four minutes in the fashion of a pissoir. Stripped naked, I was heartily glad of the downpour, for I had sweated fairly profusely in my walk up the mountain. Clearly the liquid coming down on my head was essentially water, but it had a soapy feel about it. I stood up to about half a dozen bouts, in which I washed out my clothes as best I could. Then I carried the whole dripping caboodle back to my box. It would take several hours, I thought, for the heavier garments, particularly the trousers, to dry out, so I resolved to try for some sleep. As I dozed off I wondered what items I might lack for in this singular situation. I had no razor, but then why not grow a beard? By the greatest good fortune I always carry a small pair of scissors in my rucksack. At least I could eat, keep clean, and cut my nails.

I slept much longer than I intended, nearly ten hours. When I awoke I noticed the box door, cell door if you like, was open. Before touring again through the passageways, or patronizing the privy with its remarkable drenching qualities, I tested the metal oven door. A new platter was there, piled high with the same vegetable marrow stuff.

My clothes were snuff dry. So the humidity had to be quite low, as I had thought was probably the case. I trotted along to the showers in my underpants only, for these would easily be dried should I misjudge the pissoir. Fortunately the panel was open, and it remained open from that time on, so far as I am aware, so I waited for the flush, then darted in and darted out before the thing fired itself for the next occasion. At the best of times my mountaineering clothes are distinctly rough. After their recent wetting and drying they were now baggy and down-at-heel in the extreme. I saw no point in putting on my boots and simply went barefoot, rather like a shipwrecked mariner.

I padded along the passage knowing that sooner or later I would reach the "cathedral," as I had come to think of the big rectangular box. Another box was open, different certainly from mine, and different, I thought, from that of Giselda Horne. I was just on the point of stepping inside when a voice behind me said "hello" in a foreign accent. I turned to find an Indian of uncertain middle age standing there. He stared rather wildly for perhaps thirty seconds and reached for support against the wall. To my surprise he went on, "It is not the stomach sickness. It is a matter of shock to see you, sir, for I attended a lecture you gave in Bombay last year. Professor Wycombe is it?"

"I did give a lecture in Bombay. You were in the audience?"

"Yes, but you will not remember me. It was a rather large audience. Daghri is my name, sir."

We shook hands. "You have been in the big room, sir?"

"Yes, many times."

"Recently, sir?"

"Yesterday. That is to say, before I slept. Perhaps ten hours ago."

"Then you will find it has changed."

Daghri and I hurried along the passages until we emerged into the cathedral. On the walls now were a mass of points of light, stars obviously. The projection onto the flat surfaces introduced distortions, of course, but this apart we were looking up at a complete representation of the heavens, both hemispheres.

"What does it mean, sir?" whispered the Indian.

For the moment I made no attempt to answer this critical question. I asked Daghri to tell me how he came to be there. He said he remembered walking out in the evening in the Indian countryside. Then suddenly, in a flash, it seemed, he was in this big cathedral room. It appeared almost as if he had walked around a corner in the road to find himself, not in the countryside anymore, but right there in the middle of this room, more or less at the exact spot where I myself had wakened.

Accepting that both Daghri and I were sane, there could only be one explanation. "Daghri, it must be that we are in some enormous spaceship. This display here on the walls represents the view from the ship. We're seeing the pilot's view out into space."

"My difficulty with that thought, sir, is to find the Sun."

I pointed to the bright patch lighting the entrance to the passageway. "That I think must be the Sun."

"Is there any way to make sure of this, sir?"

"Quite easily. All we need do is sit and watch. The motion of the ship, if we are in a ship, must produce changes in the planets. We only need to watch the brighter objects."

Within half an hour we had it, the apparent motion of the Earth itself, for the Earth-Moon combination was easy to pick out, once you looked in the right direction. Within an hour or so we had Venus and Mars, and already we knew the rough direction we were traveling–toward the constellation of Scorpius. We also knew the approximate speed of the ship, something above two thousand miles an hour. Reckoning the ship to be accelerating smoothly, and trusting to time from my watch, I was able to check the acceleration itself. It was quite close to ordinary gravity, a bit larger than gravity as I calculated it. This might well be the difference I had noticed in my legs right at the beginning.

It was while we were thus watching the display on the walls of the cathedral that the others slowly filtered in, one by one over a period of about five hours. The first to appear was a sandy-haired man going a bit thin on top. He announced himself as being of the name Bill Bailey, a butcher from Rotherham, Yorkshire, and where the hell was he, he'd like to know, and where was the bacon and eggs, and who was the bird he'd seen in the bloody showers, half-naked she was, but he didn't object to that, the more naked the better so far as he was concerned. For a badly frightened man it was a good performance. Although I never took to Bill Bailey, the never-ending stream of ribald remarks which issued from his lips served in the months ahead to lighten a thoroughly grim situation, at any rate so far as I was concerned.

There were two other men and four women, making a total of nine captives. Of the whole nine of us, only two had been acquainted before, Giselda Horne and Ernst Schmidt, a German industrialist. Schmidt and the girl's father were in the same line of business, meat-packing, and Schmidt had been visiting the Horne family in Chicago. He and Giselda had been swimming in the household pool when the "snatch," as I liked to call it, had taken place. Schmidt had suddenly found himself in the central part of the "cathedral," clad only in his swimming trunks. Giselda had found herself in one of the cell-like boxes attired in her dressing gown. Schmidt was pretty mad about the trunks, for obviously there was no chance of him acquiring any decent clothes here. Since we were not permitted to touch each other, since the temperature in the ship was a dry seventy degrees or thereabouts, there really wasn't any logical reason for clothes. Nevertheless, I could see Schmidt's point. I gave him the anorak out of my rucksack.

Although it was no doubt ludicrous to do so, he was glad to wear it.

Jim McClay was a tall, wiry Australian sheep farmer of about thirty-five. He had been snatched while out on his farm driving a Land Rover. Then he too was suddenly in the middle of the cathedral. The experience had very naturally knocked a good deal of the spring and bounce out of the man. But the confidence would soon return. I could see it would return by the way he was looking at Giselda Horne. She was a natural for the Australian, tall, too, and well-muscled.

Bill Bailey greeted each of the four women in his own broad style. For Giselda Horne, in a cleaned dressing gown, it was no more than a terse, "Take it off, love, come in an' cool down."

He didn't get far with Hattie Foulds, a farmer's wife from northern Lancashire. To his, "Come in, love, come right in 'ere by me. Come in to mi lap an' smoulder," she instantly retorted with, "Who's this bloody great bag of wind?"

Nevertheless, it was clear from the beginning that Hattie Foulds and Bill Bailey made a "right" pair. As the days and weeks passed, they made every conceivable attempt to get into physical contact with each other. It became a part of our everyday existence to walk past some spot from which the sound of violent retching emerged. The other women affected disgust, but I suspect their lives would also have been the poorer without these strange sexio-gastronomic outbursts. Bailey never ceased to talk about it. "Can't even match your fronts together before it hits you," he would say, "but we've got to keep on trying. Rome wasn't built in a day."

The two remaining women were much the most interesting to me. One was an Englishwoman, a face I had seen before somewhere. When I asked her name, she simply said she had been christened "Leonora Mary" and that we were to call her what we pleased. She came in that first day wearing a full-length mink coat. She was moderately tall, slender, dark with fine nose and mouth. A long wolf whistle from Bailey was followed by, "Enjoy yer shower, baby?"

This must be the woman Bailey had seen. She must have got herself trapped in the deluge exactly as I had done. With most of her clothing wet she was using the mink coat as a covering.

The remaining woman was Chinese. She came in wearing a neat smock. She looked silently from one to another of us, her face like stone. Under her imperious gaze, Bailey cracked out with, "Eee, look what we've got 'ere. 'Ad yer cherry plucked, love?"

They wanted to know about the stars, about the way Daghri and I figured out where we were going and so on and so forth. As the hours and days passed we watched the planets move slowly across the walls. We watched the inner planets getting fainter and fainter while Jupiter hardly seemed to change. But after three weeks even Jupiter was visibly dimming. The ship was leaving the solar system.

Of all these things everybody understood something. It was wonderful to see how suddenly acute the apparently ignorant became as soon as they realized the extent to which their fate depended on these astronomical matters. Throughout their lives the planets had been remote, recondite things. Now they were suddenly as real to everybody as a sack of potatoes, more real, I thought, for I doubted if any of us would ever see a potato again (erroneously, as it turned out).

Of the Einstein time dilatation, they could make out nothing at all, however. It was beyond them to understand how in only a few years we could reach distant stars. I just had to tell them to accept it as a fact. Where were we going, they all wanted to know. As if I could answer such a question! All I could say was that we had somehow been swept up by a raiding party, similar to our own parties rounding up animals for a zoo. It all fitted. Wasn't this exactly the kind of setup we ourselves provided for animals in a zoo? The boxes to sleep in, the regular food, the restrictions on mating, the passages and the cathedral hall to exercise in?

My longest conversations were with Daghri and with the aristocratic Mary. Mary and I found that so long as we kept about three feet apart we could go pretty well anywhere together at any time without falling into the troubles which were constantly afflicting Bill Bailey and Hattie Foulds. Quite early on, Mary wanted to know why we were so hermetically sealed inside this place. Animals in a terrestrial zoo can at least *see* their captors, she pointed out. They breathe the same air, they glower at each other from opposite sides of the same bars. Not in the snake house or the fish tank, I answered. *We* look in on snakes, we look in on fish, but it is doubtful if either look out on us in any proper sense. Only for birds and mammals is there much in the way of reciprocity in a terrestrial zoo. Mary burst out, "But snakes are dangerous."

"So may we be. Oh, not with poison like snakes, perhaps with bacteria. This place may be a veritable horror house so far as our captors are concerned."

I was much worried about the Chinese girl, Ling was her name, for she had the problem of language to contend with as well as the actual situation. It was also very clear that Ling intended to be harshly uncooperative. I asked Mary to do what she could to break the ice. Mary reported that Ling "read" English but didn't speak it, not yet. Gradually as the days passed, we managed to thaw out the girl to some small degree. The basic trouble was that Ling had been a politician of quite exalted status in one of the Chinese provinces. She had been a person of real consequence, not in virtue of birth, but from her own determination and ability. She gave orders and she expected obedience from those around her. Her glacial attitude to us all was a general expression of contempt for the degenerate West.

Our clothes, while easily cleaned in the showers, became more and more battered and out of shape as time went on. We dressed as lightly as possible consistent with modesty, a commodity variable from person to person. One day Bill Bailey, clad only in underpants, came into the cathedral, threw himself on the floor and said, "Oo, what a bitch! A right bitch, that. Used to run real cockfights back on the farm, illicit-like. She'd take on any half-dozen men after a fight. Says it used to key her up, put her in tone. That's what we need 'ere, Professor, a bloody great cockfight."

Ling, who was standing nearby, looked down at Bailey. "That is the sort of man who should be whipped, hard and long. In *my* town he would have been whipped for all the people to see."

The girl's expression was imperious, although her voice was quiet. Because of this, because also of her curious accent and use of words–which I have not attempted to imitate–the others, particularly Bailey, did not realize what she had said. To me the girl's attitude demanded action. I took her firmly by the arm and marched her along the passages until we came to the first open cell. Strangely enough, this action induced no sense of sickness in either of us. "Now see here, Ling, you're not in China anymore. We're all *captives* in this place. We've got to keep solidly together, otherwise we're lost. It's our only strength, to give support to each other. If it means putting up with a man like Bailey, you've just got to do it."

Even in my own ears this sounded flat and feeble, which is always the way with moderation and reason; it always sounds flat and feeble compared to an unrelenting fanatic or bigot. Certainly Ling was not impressed. She looked me over coolly, head to toe, and made the announcement, "The time will come when it will be a pity you are not ten years younger."

I was taking this as a left-handed compliment when she added, "I shall choose the Australian."

"I think you'll have trouble from the American girl."

Ling laughed–I suppose it was a laugh. The eyes, I noticed, were an intense green, the teeth a shining white. The girl must be using the soapy solution in the shower baths. It tasted pretty horrible but it allowed one to clean away the vegetable marrow food on which we were obliged to subsist.

I gave it up. The best I could see in Ling's point of view was that her ideology represented a last link with Earth. Perhaps it was her way of keeping sane, but it was entirely beyond me to understand it. I was much more impressed at the way Ling always contrived to look neat, always in the same smock.

We were undereating, because unless you were actively hungry there was no point in consuming the tasteless vegetable marrow stuff. It was mushy with a lot of moisture in it. Even so, I was surprised we managed without needing to drink, for there was no possibility of drinking the one source of fluid, the liquid in the shower bath. I could only think we were generating a lot of water internally, by oxidizing the vegetable marrow material. Every now and then we had an intense desire to chew something really hard. I used to bite away at the cord from my rucksack, often for an hour at a time.

The natural effect of the undereating was that we were nearly all losing weight. I had lost most of the excess ten pounds or so which I never seemed to get rid of back on Earth. Ernst Schmidt had lost a lot more, so much in fact that he had discarded my anorak. He went around now only in the bathing trunks which he had tightened in quite a bit. Getting fit had become a passion with the German. He had taken to running through the passages according to a systematic schedule, ten laps from the cathedral and back again for every hour he was awake. Sometimes I accompanied him, to give my muscles a little exercise, but I could never be so regular about it. He commented on this one day.

"A strange difference of temperament, Professor. We often have these little runs together, but you can't quite keep them up. Of course, I understand you have not the same need as I. But even if you had the need, you couldn't keep them up. No, I think not."

"Personal temperament?"

"It is an interesting question. Both personal and national, I think. A misleading thing in politics—and in business—is the description given to your people. Anglo-Saxons, eh? What is an Anglo-Saxon, Professor, a sort of German, maybe?"

"We're always supposed to be a kind of first cousins. There's the similarity of language, for one thing."

"Accidental, imposed by a handful of conquerors. Look at me. I speak English, if you will pardon me, I speak it with an American accent. Does that make me an American? Obviously not. I speak this way because Americans have conquered my particular world, the business world."

"Go on."

"It is a pity we have no mirrors in this place. If we had a mirror, let me tell you how you would see yourself. You would see a tallish man, with a fair skin, a big red beard, and blue eyes. You would see a Celt, not a German. Your people are Celts, Professor, not Germans, and that is the true source of the difference in our temperaments, you and I."

"So you think it goes a long way back?"

"Three thousand years or more, to the time when we Germans threw you Celts out of Europe. Yes, we understand a lot about each other, you and I, but we understand each other because we have fought each other for a long time now, not because we are the same."

I was surprised at the turn of the conversation. Schmidt must have noticed something of this in my face. "Ah, you wonder how I can tell you these things? Because these things are my real interest, not the packing of meat, for who should be interested in the packing of meat?"

"What does all this lead you to?"

"We Germans can pursue a goal relentlessly to the end. You Celts can never do so. You have what I think is called an easygoing streak. It was this streak which made the Romans admire you so much in ancient times. But it was this weakness which very nearly cost you the whole of Europe, my friend."

"To be easygoing can mean reserve, you know, reserve energy in times of real crisis."

"Ah, you are thinking of winning the last battle. It was like that in each of the wars of this century, wasn't it? You won the last battles, you won those wars. Yet from victory each time you emerged weaker than before. We Germans emerged each time stronger, even from defeat."

"Because of a tenacity of purpose?"

"Correct, Professor."

"What is it you are really telling me, Herr Schmidt? That in whatever should lie ahead of us, you will come out best?"

"A leader will emerge among us. It will be a man, an intelligent man. This leaves the choice between the two of us. Of the others, the one is a buffoon, the other a simple countryman. Which of us it will be, I am not sure yet."

"Don't be too easygoing, Herr Schmidt. You contradict yourself."

Schmidt laughed. Then he became more serious.

"In a known situation, a German will always win. He will win because all his energies are directed to a clear-cut purpose. In an unknown situation, it is all much less sure."

I mention these events in some detail because there were three points in them which came together. Hattie Foulds and her cockfights, Ling and the whipping she would have liked to administer on the person of Bill Bailey, and now Schmidt's reference to himself as a meat-packer. It made a consistent theory, except for one very big snag, Daghri. I had a long serious talk with the Indian. He denied all my suggestions with such poise and dignity that I felt I simply must believe his protestations of innocence. My theory just had to be wrong. I became depressed about it. Mary noticed the depression, she wanted to know what it was all about. I decided to tell her of the things in my mind.

"Everyone of us is affecting an attitude, or considering some problem," I began.

"How do you know? About me, for instance."

"You are considering the moral problem of whether you should permit yourself to bear children into captivity."

Mary looked me full in the face and nodded.

"My problem from the beginning," I went on, "has been to understand something of the psychology of the creatures running this ship. Zoomen, is the way I like to think of them. What the hell are they doing and why? Obviously taking samples of living creatures, perhaps everywhere throughout the Galaxy."

"You mean there might be animals from other planets on this ship?"

"Quite certainly, I would think. Through the walls of this cathedral, through the passage walls there will be other 'quarters,' other rooms and passages with other specimens in them."

"Literally, a zoo!"

"Literally. Yet my curiosity about those other compartments and their contents is less than my curiosity about the human content of this particular compartment. There are nine of us, four of us from the British Isles, an American girl, a Chinese girl, an Indian, a German, and an Australian. What kind of a distribution is that? Seven out of nine white. Can you really believe interstellar zoomen have a color prejudice?"

"Perhaps it wasn't easy to grab people, they took the first they could get."

"Doesn't hold water. Geographically, they snatched us from places as wide apart as Europe, America, India, Australia, and China. They snatched McClay, Daghri, and myself from the quiet countryside, they took you from the busy streets of London, Ling from a crowded town, Schmidt and Giselda Horne from the suburbs of Chicago. It doesn't seem as if the snatching process presented the slightest difficulty to them."

"Have you any idea of how it was done?"

"Not really. I just visualize it like picking up bits of fluff with a vacuum cleaner. They simply held a nozzle over you and you disappeared into the works."

"To come out in this place."

"It must have been something like that. Where had we got to, this color business. Differences in color might seem very unimportant to these zoomen. We only see these differences, like the differences between you and Ling, because an enormous proportion of the human brain is given over to the analysis of what are really extremely fine distinctions. It could be the zoomen hardly notice these distinctions, and if they do they don't think them worth bothering about."

"Then perhaps there was some other method of choice?"

"Must have been. If humans were snatched at random, a good half would be yellow or black. You'd only get a distribution as queer as this one if you had some system or other. But not a color system."

"Sounds like a contradiction."

"Not necessarily. Right at the beginning it occurred to me that justice might be the criterion."

"Justice!"

"Look, if *you* were taking a number of humans into lifelong captivity, it might occur to you to choose the very people who had themselves shown the least feeling for the captivity of other animals, or for the lives of other animals."

"My coat!"

"Yes, your mink coat must have marked you out from the crowd in the street. The zoomen spotted it, and at the blink of an eye you were into their vacuum cleaner."

Mary shuddered and then smiled wryly.

"I always thought of it as such a beautiful coat, warm and splendid to look at. You really believe it was the coat? I only use it for a pillow now."

"A lot of things fit the same picture. Schmidt was a meat-packer. Giselda Horne's father was in the same business, stuffing bloody bits of animals into tins."

Mary was quite excited, her own plight forgotten as the puzzle fitted into place. "And McClay reared the animals, and Bailey was a butcher, an actual slaughterer."

"And the cockfights for Hattie Foulds."

"But what about you, and Ling, and Daghri?"

"Leave me out of it. I can make a good case against myself. Ling and Daghri are the critical ones. You see, there isn't much animal-eating among Asiatic populations, really because they haven't enough in the way of feeding stuffs to be able to rear animals for slaughter. This seemed to me to be the reason why only two Asiatic people had been taken. It occurred to me that possibly even these two might have been chosen in some other way."

"What about Ling?"

"Well, to Ling people are no more than animals. I've little doubt Ling has had many a person whipped at her immediate discretion, at her pleasure even, for all I know."

"And Daghri?"

"Daghri is the contradiction, the disproof of everything. Daghri is a Hindu. Hinduism is a complicated religion, but one important part of it forbids the eating of animals."

"Perhaps Daghri doesn't have much use for that aspect of his religion."

"Exactly what I thought. I charged him with it directly, more or less accusing him of some form of violence against either animals or humans. He denied it with the utmost dignity."

"Maybe he was lying."

"Why should he lie?"

"Perhaps because he's ashamed. You know, Daghri is different in another way. What odds would you give of taking nine people at random and of finding none of them with strong religious beliefs?"

"Very small, I would imagine."

"Yet none of us has strong religious beliefs, except Daghri."

I saw exactly what Mary meant. To Daghri, religion might be no more than a sham. Perhaps the Indian was no more than a gifted liar.

Not long after this conversation Daghri disappeared. For a while I thought he had retired, possibly in shame, to his box-like cell. In one of my runs with Schmidt I noticed all the cells open. Daghri was not to be found in any one of them. We searched high and low, but Daghri simply was not there. "High and low" is an obvious exaggeration, for there wasn't any possible hiding place in our aseptic accommodation. It was rather that we looked everywhere many times. Daghri was gone. The general consensus was that the poor fellow had been abstracted by the zoomen for "experiments." I was of a similar mind at first, then it all clicked into place. I rushed into the cathedral. The others quickly followed, so we were assembled there, eight of us now. I studied the star pattern on the wall. We hadn't bothered with it of late, treating it more as a decoration than as a source of information.

What a fool I'd been! I should have noticed the slight shift of the patterns back to their original forms. Owing to the motion of the ship, the stars had moved very slightly, but now they had moved back. The planets were there, too, the planets of our own solar system. The double Earth-Moon was there. So was the sunlight replacing artificial light at the entrance of the passageways—there was a small subtle difference.

"We're being taken back," I heard someone say.

I knew we were not being taken back. Daghri had been taken back, the contradiction had been removed. My instinct had been right, Daghri had been telling the truth. Daghri had ill-treated no animal, Daghri was saved, but not so the rest of us. The planets moved across the wall, just as they had done before. We were on our way out again.

The others couldn't believe it at first, then they didn't want to believe it, but at last as the hours passed they were forced to believe it. Disintegration set in quickly. Giselda Horne gave way badly. She seemed big and strong but really she was only an overdeveloped kid. I thought she might be better alone, so I took her back to her own cell. She nodded and went in. Silently, from behind me, Ling glided after Giselda Horne. I shouted to Ling to come out and leave the girl alone. Ling turned with a look of haughty indifference on her face. At that very moment the panel of the cell closed. There was just a fleeting fraction of a second in which I saw the expression on Ling's face change from indifference to triumph.

The others gathered outside the cell. We could hear nothing from inside, for the panel was completely soundproof. The Chinese girl had judged the situation quite exactly. Giselda Horne was near the edge of sanity. With cutting and sadistic words, and with the force of an intense personality, Ling would push her over that edge.

The panel slid open. Horror-stricken, I gazed inside. Horror dissolved to laughter. Gone was Ling's neat smock. Blood was oozing from long scratches on Giselda Horne's face. Ling had evidently fought catlike, as I would have anticipated. Giselda Horne had fought in a different style. One swinging fist must have hit Ling on the mouth, for now it was puffy and bleeding. A fist had also whacked the Chinese girl a real beauty on the left eye. Ling staggered out, leaving Giselda Horne with a big smile on her face.

"Gee, that was real good," said the American girl.

It was two days, two waking and sleeping periods, before I saw Ling again. She still contrived to appear reserved and haughty, even though the furious set-to had left her with the blackest eye I ever saw and with hardly any remnants of clothing.

"The American girl and I, we will share the Australian," Ling said. "It is a pity you are not five years younger," she added.

Mary took it all with a great calmness. "I had become reconciled to it, captivity, I mean. This really proves the zoomen have a sense of justice, to go back all that way to put Daghri home again."

Somehow I couldn't tell Mary. I knew the zoomen hadn't made any mistake about Daghri. It was an experiment, done quite deliberately to see how we would react. The zoomen just couldn't have read me so accurately and Daghri so badly. With Daghri gone, we made eight, four couples—the animals came into the Ark. Another thing, choose a smallish number. Being an irrational creature, a human might say, 7. A really rational creature would always choose a binary number, 8.

Mary put a hand lightly on my arm. "You never said what it was *you* had done."

"My sin was the worst of you all. My sin was that I was a consumer. I ate the poor creatures McClay reared on his farm, the animals Bailey slaughtered, the bloody bits Schmidt stuffed into tins."

"But millions do the same. I did, everybody does!"

"Yes, but they know not what they do. *I* knew what I was doing. For twenty years now I've been clear in my mind about it. Yet I've gone on taking the line of least resistance. I made minor adjustments, like eating more fish and less meat, but I never faced the real problem. I knew what I was doing."

The weeks passed, then the months. Long ago, Mary and I had begun to share the same cell for sleeping. We had no trouble with the sickness, even when we shared my rucksack for a pillow. The same favor was not immediately extended to the others. The favor perhaps was granted because I had kept my small scrap of knowledge about the zoomen strictly to myself.

The day did come, however, when the others were allowed into physical contact. There was no mistaking the day, for Bill Bailey appeared in the cathedral clad only in his now tattered underpants, shouting, "Bloody miracle. We got on last night, real good and proper." Then he was off, high-stepping, knees up, like a boxer trotting along the road. Round and round the cathedral he went chanting, "Raw eggs, raw eggs, mother. Oh, for a bloody basin of raw eggs."

Giselda Horne was standing nearby. "What does it mean?" she asked rather shyly.

"It means, my dear, that we're only nine months away from our destination," I answered.

This narrative was discovered in curious circumstances many many years after it was written, indeed long long after it had become impossible to identify the particular mountain mentioned by its author, Meall Ghaordie.

ZOOMEN

Landing on a distant planetary system, the crew of the fifth deep interstellar mission were astonished to discover what seemed like a remarkable new species of humanoid. The language spoken by the creatures was quite unintelligible in its details, but in the broad pattern of its sounds it was strikingly similar to an archaic human language.

The creatures lived a wild, nomadic existence. Yet they were imbued with a strong religious sense, a religion apparently centering around a "covenant," guarded day and night in a remote stronghold. It was there, in a remote mountain valley, that the creatures assembled for their most solemn religious ceremonies. By a technologically advanced subterfuge, access to the "covenant" was at length obtained. It turned out to be the story of the "Professor," reproduced above without emendations or omissions. It was written in a small book of the pattern of an ancient diary. This it was the creatures guarded with such abandoned ferocity, although not a word of it did they understand.

The manuscript has undoubtedly created many more problems than it has solved. What meaning can be attached to the fanciful anatomical references? What was "Munro-bagging"? These questions are still the subject of bitter debate among savants. Who were the sinister zoomen? Could it be that the Professor and his party turned out to be too hot to handle, in a biological sense, of course, and that the zoomen were forced to dump them on the first vacant planet? The pity is that the "Professor" did not continue his narrative. His writing materials must soon have become exhausted, for the above narrative almost fills his small diary.

It was the appearance of the creatures which misled the fifth expedition into thinking they were dealing with humanoids, not humans. It was the unique combination of flaming red hair with intense green, Mongoloid eyes. Did these characteristics become dominant in the mixed gene pool of the Professor's party, or was the true explanation more direct and elementary?

PYM MAKES HIS POINT

"Geordie" Jones mopped his brow. He had been so nicknamed by Welsh relatives, scornful of his residence in one of the new T.V.-aerial-decked housing estates of Newcastle-on-Tyne. He finished his cup of tea and told his mate, Barney O'Connor–the only honest Irishman, according to himself–it was time she was moving. "She" was the Royal Scotsman. They walked the long platform of Waverley Street Station, Edinburgh, saying little except that it was bloody hot. Which was true, it was 95° F. or 35° C. It was exactly the same whichever way you looked at it, bloody hot. Come to think of it, why did the bloody newspapers and the bloody T.V. always go on about 35° C. or 95° F.? Geordie Jones had worked with steam engines all his life. He knew perfectly well about C.

and F. Why did the bloody newspapers give themselves such airs, as if they were the only ones who knew anything at all?

In truth, it was both hot and humid. It was the sort of summer spell which few people outside the British Isles believe possible as far north as 55° latitude. It wasn't quite as hot or as unpleasant as the East Coast of the United States can be in summer, ex-air-conditioning. But it was more than hot enough for the cabin of a big Diesel locomotive to be avoided by those in a position to avoid it. The sooner they were moving and picking up speed the better it would be, grunted Geordie.

They drove the old tub as hard as she would go east into Lothian. The miles flew by. In less than an hour they had turned southeast for Berwick. Quite suddenly, there was an enormous fall of temperature. Not ten degrees, not twenty, either F. or C., but right down as if they were running into winter. Incredibly, snow flakes appeared on the windscreen and they had to start the wipers. Within ten minutes, Geordie Jones brought the train to a grinding, shrieking halt. Ahead of them was an enormous snowdrift. Looking out, Barney reported a blizzard to be raging. Fifteen minutes later, the train was entirely snowed in. To Geordie Jones, to Barney O'Connor, to every passenger on the train, it seemed as if the world had gone daft. It was bloody insane, but then neither Geordie Jones nor Barney O'Connor knew anything of the dealings of Professor Pym.

Pym was retired now from one of the smaller universities in the north of England. For twenty-five years he had worked hard to organize the department of physics for the benefit of his staff and for the sake of the apparently unending stream of undergraduates. He had struggled to do what research he could in spare moments, in the depths of vacations mostly. He had managed several useful pieces of work, although nothing at all distinguished had fallen into his lap.

Professor Pym and his wife lived economically in a small house in a not very attractive suburb of the town—economically, in part so they could give help to a married daughter with a young family, in part for them to afford the cottage they had bought in Hartsop Village, Patterdale, in the Lake District. Time passes, with results more tragic to the old than the young. The daughter had gone with her husband to Australia because there were better opportunities in the vibrant young Commonwealth. When Pym's wife died in her seventieth year he was left, still with many friends and acquaintances, but without anyone of close attachment. In many ways, life had become a memory.

It was natural for Pym to give up his suburban home, to retire to Patterdale, to the hills he loved, his last love really. Now approaching the middle seventies, he was still to be seen out walking on a fine afternoon. Given time, he could still manage the broad grassy tracks leading up from the valley to the higher slopes. His weather-beaten face, white hair, and shy, diffident smile were well known to the locals. Although he wasn't one of them, they made him feel welcome in the village.

Lately, Pym hadn't been any too well. It could be just the hot spell, of course, quite exceptionally hot it was. Yet a bit of heat shouldn't bother him this much, or cause him active pain. He should see a doctor—but then why? Either he was seriously ill or he wasn't. If it was bad they'd only rush him into hospital, to a little cubicle of a room. The doctors might drag out his life for a month or two, but what were a few extra months worth, spent looking at walls and a ceiling, compared to a last walk along the valley? Besides, there was a piece of work he ought to finish.

Pym did in fact finish his work. It put quite a drain on his failing strength, but he finished it. Then he sat himself out in the garden, relaxing. A stranger came down the hill path from the direction of "The Knott." In a few minutes he was at the cottage. Then he paused for a moment, nodded, and opened the garden gate. Pym saw a man of about thirty, handsome in a slightly repellent way, coming up the garden path. "Do you think you could make me a pot of tea?"

Pym rose slowly from his wicker chair. "Of course, if you

wouldn't mind having it inside. You see, it's a bit awkward to carry the things out here."

Pym showed the stranger into the tiny sitting room and then went to put on the kettle. When he came back with the tea he found the fellow reading his latest paper. It seemed a bit impudent, but Pym didn't like to be too impolite. "Are you a scientist, might I ask?"

"You could call me that, Professor Pym."

"So you know my name?"

"You are well known around here."

"Not really."

"Oh, yes. There aren't many scientists in these parts, real scientists. Let me ask you a question, Professor Pym. Do you consider yourself a real scientist?"

Pym flopped into a chair. "That hardly seems very civil."

The stranger threw back his head and laughed. His teeth were evenly spaced, very white, and apparently without blemishes. Pym liked him less and less, particularly as he went on, "You are a Fellow of the Institute of Physics. I know that. It doesn't answer my question. Take this paper here, for instance. It is no better, no worse, than the fifty-three other papers you have written. In it you make six assumptions each reasonably plausible in itself. But have you ever paused to reflect that a chain of six assumptions gives only a poor chance of the whole argument being right? In fact, your paper is wrong. It is utterly worthless."

Pym went very white, his legs trembled badly. "You can't know that! Even if you've worked on the subject yourself, it's impossible to be sure."

For answer, the stranger took three sheets of paper from his rucksack. He flicked them down in front of the old man. "Read these and you will see."

The writing was small and neat and the pages were well-filled. Pym put on his reading glasses. Ten lines of poetry and the hand of a master is obvious, the same for ten bars of music. So it was here. Pym read on and on in growing astonishment. The logic was concise, crystal clear. It not only solved the problem along quite unexpected lines, it showed how the problem had half a dozen new connections which nobody had noticed before.

Pym was under no illusion now, no illusion that he was dealing with an ordinary walker coming down off the hills into the valley. With more calm than he felt, he came instantly to the point. "So what might be the purpose of this visit? Not a pot of tea, I see, for you haven't touched it."

"Not a pot of tea, Professor Pym."

"You still have the advantage of me."

"More than you realize. If it is a name you are seeking, some call me Death. To a scientist this might seem unduly melodramatic. Yet there is a component of truth in it. See."

The stranger walked to the window. The sunshine vanished outside. Pym felt his mouth bone dry. He could see the gaunt hills of winter, his hills, with the grass and bracken and flowers gone, with the sky overcast. An instant later the Sun flashed out and it was summer again. The stranger resumed his seat. "I have other names. Some call me the Devil, also rather melodramatic, I am afraid. Yet there is a component of the truth in this, too. To be blunt, Professor Pym, I am here to bargain with you."

To his own surprise, Pym was amused. "Mephistopheles—Dr. Faustus! You don't expect me to take that old stuff seriously."

The stranger smiled in return. "How times change. Ah, well, new men, new methods. No, I am not going to offer any fair Marguerite. On a simple calculation, you have earned sufficient over the past thirty years to have bought yourself quite enough in that direction, if you had been so inclined. Say an average of twenty-five hundred pounds per annum, giving a total of seventy-five thousand pounds. Fair Marguerites don't come as expensive as that, Professor. Give me credit for a little intelligence."

"Suppose you tell me what you have to offer."

"Not so fast. Before I make any offer, I intend to touch on a few sensitive points. Take the manner of your election to the Institute of Physics, for instance. Aha, I see we have a reaction there. Let me remind you of the things you have tried so hard to forget. Shall I recite the names of the committee that recommended your election, the names of your friends? Of course they did nothing grossly improper. They didn't push you ahead of any much better man. What they did—your friends—was to push you ahead of ten other men of equal ability."

"Stop it! For God's sake, can't you spare me anything? I'm old now, and tired."

"Yet you are ambitious. You have written still another worthless paper, even though the writing of it has consumed many of the last days of your life. Why did you write this rubbish? Don't insult me with nonsense about your duty as a scientist. You know standards as well as I do. You wrote this paper in a last vain hope of pulling something off. You wrote it in the spirit of a gambler who must have one last fling."

Pym was trembling again. "In pity's name, come to the point."

"I have no pity. I have already told you who I am. How far are you willing to gamble, Professor Pym?"

"What must I offer?"

"Should I say your soul? No, no, we don't believe in souls nowadays. Your life, the remainder of your life. The disease that will kill you is even now at work. You already know it. If you send me away from here you will live until winter descends on the hills, until the precise moment I showed to you a while ago. The last days of the summer will be clear and beautiful. These you will have, without too much pain. You will walk the valley and you will climb the lower hills once again."

"The alternative?"

"Immediate death. These last days, Professor, the beauty

and pathos of these last days. That is what I bargain for."

"And the offer?"

"The paper, the three sheets which you have just read. You will copy them and seal them in an envelope addressed to the Institute of Physics. You may trust me to see it reaches its destination. I am no defaulter on a bargain."

"Will you answer me a question before I decide?"

"You may ask it."

"What possible advantage do you get out of this arrangement? I'm going to die anyway, so why not wait? It must come to the same thing from your point of view."

The stranger smiled. "I am pleased with the question, Professor. I will gladly answer it. If you accept the bargain, I shall get nothing at all from it. *You* will be the gainer. These papers will come as a thoroughly worthwhile final achievement to your life. You will go out with a bang, not a whimper. Understand, I make no claim that what I am giving is great physics. It is not a major new theory, nor need it be for your purpose. It is a thoroughly sound piece of craftsmanship, exactly the kind of thing you have always had the ambition to achieve."

In a considerable measure, Pym had now recovered his wits. He was puzzled. "So either way you get nothing out of it. If I refuse you get nothing, if I accept you get nothing."

The stranger considered the matter for a while. Then he said, "It hardly behooves me to explain my motives. Yet I will say this: I am gambling you will not yield a single day, a single hour, in exchange for the paper. You will cling to life until the ultimate moment."

"Surely it's my own affair if I decide to refuse?"

The stranger was reluctant to answer, so Pym plunged on. "Considering the advantages on your side, I don't think you're showing up very well."

At this, Pym's tormentor bared his white teeth and snapped, "Professor Pym, as a physicist you know events are not lost. They exist, always. They remain for those with the power to recover them, just as a film of past events can remain after those events have taken place. I want a film of you, Professor, clinging to life, clinging to the last, tedious moment, in a negation of everything you claim to be."

Pym felt a sudden tautness. He was in a trap with his retreat cut off. The only possibility was to attack. "If it's so important to you, I think you must be prepared to stake a lot more than these three sheets."

Pym's effrontery took the stranger by surprise. He indicated the papers, his eyes flashing. "These are all you will get from me, unless you are prepared to gamble very much more than the last days of your life."

The waters were rapidly deepening.

"What have you in mind?" asked Pym.

"You, Professor Pym, you must be the stake. If you want to play games with me."

"What do I stand to win?"

"Anything you please, anything, my friend!"

"And the wager itself?"

"I wager that, even with a completely free wish, you are incapable of specifying anything that will make a *permanent* mark on the world. These sheets here, which made our previous game, will not serve you. Nor must you be vague–you are not permitted to ask for the solution to a problem you cannot define. You must not say 'invent me a particle,' or 'give me a theory as good as Einstein's.' It is not to be as easy as that. My wager, Professor, is that in the deepest possible sense you are a failure. You can think of nothing of importance."

Pym felt as if strange, unknown muscles were tightening within him. His every instinct was to accept the challenge. He was angry now, with an inner, white-hot anger. Yet he saw clearly that if you could conceive of a problem you were already halfway to its solution. Which was the trouble with this wager. Unless you had the right concept, you just couldn't come out with any significant idea. Then a curious notion flashed through his mind. It was certain to win, quite splendid.

"I accept the wager. I will undertake to make a permanent mark on the world."

"You are free to ask whatever you wish."

Pym smiled broadly into the Devil's face.

"Without loss of life, build me a mountain range, up to thirty thousand feet in height, along the border between England and Scotland."

The Devil, seeing instantly that Pym, this pitiful little fellow, had outmaneuvered him, vanished in a flash of smoke, forgetting to take the three sheets of paper.

Geordie Jones and Barney O'Connor shivered as they waited long hours for their train to be dug out. They knew nothing of Professor Pym, nor did they know the Devil is no defaulter on a bargain.

Pym died during the winter. His last paper, easily his best, is still remembered with affection at the Institute of Physics, the "Pym Effect," as it is internationally known. But of Pym's greatest achievement, even the pundits are unaware. The British nowadays never speak about their weather. It is always bad, except miraculously in May and June, when the skies clear and Pym's mountains can be seen high in the sky, utterly remote and indescribably beautiful.

THE MAGNETOSPHERE

Francis Charles Lennox Pevensey, third son of the fourteenth Earl of Byeford, was a powerful great ox of a fellow. Home on vacation from prep school at the age of twelve, he engaged his father in a friendly wrestling bout. The fourteenth Earl was trapped unfortunately into a bear hug and had a couple of ribs broken for his pains—the ribs went off, in fact, like a pistol shot. Fortunately young Pev had an equable temperament, so events like this were quite rare.

Pev's performances in other directions were less impressive. For one thing, he was utterly and hopelessly incapable of grasping what his teachers were talking about. Languages, history, math, science, literature, all came the same to him, they rebounded without effect off his bulky frame.

Sport was like the parson's egg. He was a sucker for the bowlers at cricket. Nor did he show up particularly well at tennis. But anything that had to be thrown or heaved was simply thrown or heaved, yards and yards further than anybody else. His performances on the rugger field came near to making the game ridiculous. Once he had grasped the object of the game, to carry the ball to that place over yonder beneath those goal posts, why that was exactly what he did. He carried it to the goal posts whenever it came to him. It was all perfectly simple. His school lost no games while he played.

Public school followed prep school. Neither the psychologist, nor the leopard with its spots, will be surprised to learn that Pev showed no sign of changing in the smallest respect. In olden times, Oxford would have followed public school. Pev would have spent two or three years working under a coach for his matriculation. Meanwhile he would have chewed Cambridge to a fine mince whenever the opportunity presented itself.

With the elimination of privilege from the Oxford-Cambridge setup, this classic pattern was utterly beyond realization. Even the fourteenth Earl became reconciled at last to the idea that Oxford and Cambridge were not only crammed with bricklayers' sons but the damned bricklayers themselves were actually running the show, his old College even. The only idea which recommended itself was to send the lad to the United States, on the curious understanding that the streets of New York were paved with gold.

Following six torrid months of "business," young Pev conceived the idea of entering space school. Surprisingly, he got over the first hurdle, admission for a preliminary year. It was typical of the difference between the American and the British ways of life that the Americans admitted him on his few strong points, very strong points, whereas the British would have turned him down on his many weak ones.

Not until Pev appeared on the football field did his new career gather any aura of distinction. Sent in a few minutes before the end of the second quarter, Pev got his hands on the ball and proceeded to march fifty-five yards—for a safety. Instantly he became something of a celebrity, he had gotten himself an image. The eleven occasions that first year on which he bulled over for a touchdown did nothing to dispel the image.

His instructors were compelled to bow to the facts—his prowess on the football field, his good temper, his impeccable manners, and, above all else, that indeed he was a real, genuine English lord. In sum, they found it impossible to flunk him. Always they gave him a bare pass, always the minimum, except of course in the physical examinations. With these he had little trouble. When it came to the toughness tests, particularly acceleration tests, Pev came out at the top, not the bottom. Under 5g most people looked like rubber. He didn't, he felt the acceleration, and that was about all. The doctors said he was a freak, which seemed to him to explain a lot he hadn't understood before.

Miraculously, he graduated, very low on the list, it is true, but graduated he was nonetheless. Now he had that malicious little bit of paper, which gives nothing directly to its holder, but which will debar you utterly should you not have it. Now he was licensed to proceed. Whither, the bit of paper did not say.

Unknown to Pev, a controversy soon raged around his person. Weight for weight, how did he compare with a pile of electronic junk, taken as an all-purpose computer? Pev was chosen because he was the dumbest graduate anybody could think of. The answer turned out to be conditional on the circumstances. In well-understood situations the electronics was much better—it was better, for that matter, than the brightest graduates. In ill-understood situations, on the other hand, a human showed up more favorably. If you couldn't foresee what was going to happen, so that you had no idea at all of how to design your electronic instrument, even Pev came out ahead.

When at last the first extrasolar system mission was blasted out into distant space, Pev was included in the crew, on much this same basis. Nobody knew what to expect on a planet ten light years away. Pev's sheer brute strength might have its place. If it didn't turn out that way, the mission would hardly be prejudiced, it seemed—there was plenty of brain-power in the rest of the crew.

Monotony was the killer on the outward journey. Everybody expected trouble with time but nobody had quite realized how bad it was going to be. It was the concentration that went to pieces—you tried to read, but your attention inevitably wandered. You didn't talk, because you got to hate the others. You tried to sleep, but after a while you found you couldn't sleep properly, you kept waking every ten or twenty minutes.

In the narrow confines of the spaceship, the crew baited Pev unmercifully. It was a raw, primitive situation, with everybody pecking the unfortunate individual who happened to lie at the bottom of the order. True, Pev could have smashed any one of them in two or three massive blows, but his upbringing and his temperament forbade any such crude physical demonstration. He took it all with a smile, but it bit gradually deeper as time went slowly by. Particularly, he came to hate the navigational fixes. Naturally, he did the measurements wrong, and his reductions of the data hadn't the smallest conceivable validity in mathematics. The others forced him to do them just for the laughs. They stood around while he made the measurements, then they all examined his reduction sheets. Like an animal which learns to play up to its master, Pev learned to do the fixes in the way that seemed to amuse them most. He stood there smiling as they laughed, pitifully hoping to ingratiate himself, like a dog thumping its tail.

Once they landed on the new planet, Pev had a fair measure of revenge. Gravity turned out to be seventy percent stronger than it is on Earth. He was the only one strong enough to get around more or less normally. The others moved slowly, especially uphill, when their gait reminded Pev of climbers near the summit of Mount Everest. They panted and sweated as if their hearts and lungs were bursting, which was very nearly true. It was a pity, because the new planet was quite remarkably beautiful. There were big woolly clouds and lots of gentle, warm rain. It was wonderfully green everywhere. Shimmering streams ran down valleys glowing with brilliant flowers. There were fish in the streams. There were insects and tiny animals the size of a mouse, but no large creatures and no birds.

To Pev it was a veritable Paradise. He traveled about as much as he could, but with the others more or less incapacitated by the deadly gravitation, he couldn't venture too far away. After the cramped years in the spaceship, it was galling not to be able to cover the whole of this new world. Yet the nights made up in a large measure for Pev's disappointment. The nights were the chief glory of this new world. The sky blazed with pulsating colors, driven like lances across the heavens. Mostly there would be three or four arcs of light. They didn't stay long in the same place. New arcs would flash out like the trail of a brilliant meteorite, sometimes overhead, sometimes down near the horizon, sometimes to the right of you, sometimes to the left. You never knew where the next one would burst out. Occasionally, perhaps half a dozen times in a night, the whole sky would fill with lights, as if a huge, multicolored cosmic firecracker had suddenly gone off. It was all completely silent.

The mission was not so much concerned with esthetics, however, as with the collection of facts. Auroral activity of this very great intensity must produce strong electromagnetic signals. Receivers were set up. Sure enough, there were electromagnetic signals in plenty. The emissions were monitored carefully from day to day and it emerged that there were marked regularities. The aspects of a phased situation were revealed step by step. Incredible as it seemed, there was a controlled order in the magnetosphere of this planet. Could some form of data-processing be going on up there? Were the electrons and the magnetic field disposed in such a configuration that the vast magnetosphere, encompassing the whole planet, was behaving like a gigantic electronic brain?

The next step was for the crew to transmit electromagnetic signals themselves. This they did in the hope of receiving some response. So far as anybody could tell, either by looking directly up at the flickering sky, or from the instrumental records, there was no change. It all went on exactly the same as before. The mission continued its explorations on the ground, but there was always a return to the sky, to the problem of what was going on up there.

After their long outward journey, the men had come to feel acutely alone. Earth was now many many years away. Memories of acquaintances, even of families and friends, had become unpleasantly diffuse, as if the old life had lost reality. The spaceship had become their world. During the voyage it had seemed to each man as if the others were all there was of life, anywhere in the whole universe. The landing on this new planet had come as an indescribable relief. Even the insects were a relief. Yet the green valleys and the chuckling streams were no substitute for some form of intelligible communication. It was this the men ached for, not so much to learn something new as to feel they weren't alone. The desperate need was to get away from the feeling of isolation, of being a negligible microcosm in the vast, implacable, unyielding infinity of space and time.

Establishing contact with the wonderful thing in the sky came to have overriding importance. Then failure after failure led to a growing impatience. If only the thing would respond in some way, any way, even an answering ray of light would do, only so long as it didn't go on ignoring them. All they wanted now was the slightest sign of recognition. Yet nothing they did made the smallest difference.

Someone had the idea that perhaps their signals weren't getting through, perhaps it wasn't possible for signals to propagate directly from the ground into the magnetosphere. It could be the waves were being reflected or refracted, back to the ground again. This suggested that signals be injected directly into the magnetosphere, from the ship in orbit around the planet. Unfortunately, it meant waiting until the beginning of the homeward flight, because the captain didn't want to put the strain of a double landing on his rocket motors, not with gravity as strong as it was here. Partly because of this, and partly because of the sheer physical strain of putting up day after day with the excess weight occasioned by the gravity, the captain decided to cut short the length of the explorations on the ground.

One trouble was that nobody had any idea of the kind of response they should be looking for. Could this thing be aware of the spaceship flying right through it, any more than we ourselves are aware of some particular bacterium inside our own bodies? The electromagnetic signals they were now injecting into it should be producing some disturbance, but could the Thing be aware of the source of the disturbance? At all events, they got no more in the way of a response than before. Whatever it was, it ignored them completely.

A reaction set in. The electronic-brain fell out of favor. It began to look as though they were dealing only with some unusual natural phenomenon and not at all with an utterly new form of "life." This made a big difference, a big difference in the tactics they should adopt. They'd better quit fooling with electromagnetic signals. They'd better do something really effective to stir up the situation. A nuclear bomb exploded in the works, after the manner of the old Starfish project, was more in line with the needs of the case. Back on Earth there had been objectors to Starfish. Here there would be no objectors, thought the captain, as he set about preparations for the experiment in hand. Actually he was wrong. Pev objected, although he didn't say so. Pev didn't understand the talk about electronics, or of the need for a bomb, or about flutings in the magnetic field. What he did know was that he liked this planet, with its gentle landscape and its magnificent skies. He couldn't conceive of any reason for wanting to change it.

It was easy for Pev to make a blunder on purpose, to set the motors firing for a sweep-out from orbit. He had acquired a reputation for mistakes of all kinds. Nobody would suspect him of anything more than another stupidity. The others felt the growing acceleration. A glance at the controls made the situation clear to the captain, made it clear there would barely be enough time for them to strap themselves down before the big drive came on. The controls had gotten preset, there was no stopping it now.

Pev saw the rest of the crew safe before stowing himself away. The drive hit him harder than he ever remembered it. For the first time in his life he passed out completely. When it was all over they cursed him good and proper. He'd ruined their last chance of getting to grips with the Thing. They'd give him hell all the way home, they promised him that. Pev didn't care. He felt curiously lightheaded, he'd felt that way from the moment he became conscious again after the blackout. He felt it didn't matter, not one jot or tittle, what the other members of the crew thought about him.

Soon they got him to do a navigational fix. The mood lasted. He did it in a carefree fashion, taking the measurements quickly and stabbing down the numbers as he thought the numbers should go. Then he handed his data and his reduction sheets to the captain. Deliberately the captain ignored them —they wanted to keep him on the hook as long as possible. Somehow Pev didn't care. He knew he wouldn't care even if they laughed themselves sick about it. Sensing this, and seeing him pretty relaxed, the captain at last began to examine the papers. The others crowded around. To begin with, they all had silly grins on their faces. Then the grins were wiped clean away as they thumbed their way through Pev's reductions. At last the captain looked up and said, "Hell, I never believed that old story about the monkey typing out Shakespeare. But it's happened. It's right, the whole bloody fix, it's one hundred percent right."

A PLAY'S THE THING

The dinner had been elegantly cooked. The three who had eaten it formed an elegant trio, a handsome man in his early forties, a perhaps still more handsome woman in her middle thirties, and a girl of twenty. The girl was fair with long hair the color of ripe corn. The woman was dark with a finely chiseled nose and large, arresting eyes.

"Coffee, I think," murmured the woman.

"Excellent, my dear," said the man, "coffee would be exactly right. I had no idea you were so splendid a cook."

"I do most things well. When I have a mind to."

The girl was on her feet. "I'll fetch it."

"Let me. It would be the least I could do," offered the man.

"It would indeed be the least you could do. But let Cynthia go."

The girl with hair the color of ripe corn left the man and woman together. Nothing was said while the girl was absent. The woman seated herself against one end of a long couch, placing her well-shaped legs along the length of the couch. She was still adjusting the cushions behind her back when Cynthia returned with the coffee. It was in a fashioned silver pot. The cups were of delicate china. The girl poured the coffee and served the man and woman. Then she seated herself comfortably, the three of them forming a triangle facing each other.

The woman tasted the coffee. "Mm, almost right, a touch of salt perhaps was needed."

She sipped again reflectively, and then announced in a loud firm voice, "John, darling, you are a lousy sod."

"Not literally, I can assure you."

"Not literally, I would agree. Figuratively, shall we say?"

"You have every reason to be annoyed, I suppose."

"Darling, *annoyed* is scarcely the word for it. *Bloody furious* is much more the way I feel."

"My dear, we can't put the clock back. 'The moving finger writes,' and all that sort of thing."

"If the moving finger had confined itself to writing, we'd hardly be in this very murky situation, would we?"

"I mean, we've got to face up to things, like rational human beings."

"I fully intend to face up to things. Very rationally, my dear John, as you will presently discover. But facing up to things still doesn't stop me from being bloody furious."

"Helen," said the girl, "I just don't see how getting mad about it is going to help."

"What *is* going to help?" asked the woman.

"Nothing really, I suppose," admitted the girl.

"Time, perhaps? Is that the view you would both like me to take?"

"Oh, come now, Helen. It's not as bad as all that."

"It's happened before. It's not the end of the world."

The woman turned from the girl toward the man. She threw back her head and laughed, "Of course it's not the end of the world. I never said it was. I'm complaining much more about the *way* it was done than about *what* was done."

"You goaded me for long enough."

"Goad or no goad, there is a certain well-defined moral level below which a man in your position is not expected to stoop."

"A great deal depends on the direction from which you look at it."

"No doubt."

"I mean, you can't possibly blame me for everything."

"I blame the crucial moment on you. So I'm going to make you suffer for it, darling."

The girl fidgeted and shook her head. "I can't see any one of us being particularly to blame. We're all to blame. I asked for it and I got it."

The woman laughed again. "I didn't ask for it, yet I've got it, too, my dear."

There was a short silence. Then the woman shuffled along the couch to where she could stare directly into the man's face.

"Well, are you satisfied with what you've done to both of us, you bloody great bull?"

"Very well satisfied."

"I wonder what your academic colleagues are going to say when it all comes out? You'll smirk on the other side of your face when they chuck you out."

"Nonsense, these are private matters, outside the university's competence. If everybody were thrown out for this sort of thing, every faculty in every university in the world would be decimated tomorrow."

"There's one thing you forget. Cynthia was your student. The university won't take kindly to that, my dear John. It's morally equivalent to incest, seducing a student. They'll bounce you good and hard for it."

"But I didn't seduce Cynthia! Damn it all, there wasn't the smallest question of seduction."

The man lifted his hands toward the girl. "I said I'd look after things but you said you'd see to it."

"I said I would but I never intended to."

"In heaven's name, why not?"

"Because I wanted it to happen. I wanted you to give me a child. So it would commit me. So it would commit both of us."

"Marriage would commit both of us."

"Marriage isn't possible, not now."

"Why not?"

"Because of Helen."

"Look, Helen isn't that sort, the marrying sort. She's played the game her way. Well, she's lost for once, that's all."

"Don't be so sure," interposed the woman calmly, "the game isn't played out yet."

"You'd wanted to make Helen for a long time, hadn't you?" the girl asked the man.

"I suppose so," he admitted.

"For how long, ten years?"

"Perhaps, a long time, certainly."

"But she's the other kind, so you didn't get anywhere at all until I came along."

The girl stopped and looked to the woman. "He still doesn't understand the way it is."

"He soon will," smiled the woman. With evident pleasure, she leaned across to the man and put a hand on his knee. "Don't you see? She's the other kind, too, my kind. Cynthia is my kind. When she tricked you into making her pregnant she was trying to break it. She knew you'd have to marry her, being her teacher. She knew she'd got you in the sensitive places."

The man sucked in his breath and scowled. The woman patted his knee. "That hits your self-esteem, doesn't it? It wasn't your sex power what did it, darling. It was Cynthia thinking she'd extend the range of her interests a bit."

The girl was dreamy and reflective. "I would have tried, of

course, but I don't know whether it could ever have worked. I'd probably have regressed in the long run."

"You didn't know it was this way with Cynthia?" the man asked the woman.

For answer, she laughed deeply and quite genuinely. "Don't be such an idiot. Do you think I'd have gone off to bed with you if I'd known. I could have cut you out with a snap of the fingers if only I'd known."

"Exactly what happened between the two of you?" asked the girl.

"We've already been over it twenty times."

"I'd like to hear the story his way though."

"Oh, Helen was white-hot for you," began the man. "That can't be any news. But she thought you were hot for me."

"So you made a trade. You'd give her a chance with me, put me in her path, as it were. In exchange, she allowed you to make her."

"It was like that, more or less."

"How do you mean, more or less?" thundered the woman. "There was plenty more to it. He said he would take care of things and by God he did. If he'd been aiming to make me pregnant he couldn't have done it better."

"Then here's a surprise for you," interjected the man. "That's exactly what I was aiming to do. I'd waited long enough. You'd teased me long enough."

The woman drew in a deep breath. "Then hang on to your hat, my dear. The wind is really going to blow now."

The girl lost her dreamy look. She sat up alertly, her chin cupped in her hands. "Even so, I'd have thought it would have taken more than one weekend–unless he was *very* lucky."

The woman looked gravely across at the girl. "He discovered the right time of the month. I'm sure of it. That's the thing which makes me so mad about it all."

The girl whistled between her teeth. "That *is* pretty ultimate. He must have felt an intense need to justify himself. Biologically, I mean. I bet it's done him a world of good, getting himself rid of a bad infertility psychosis."

"Cynthia, darling, will you please be a little less ready to see his point of view? Try to develop a sense of majestic rage."

"It would go well with her coloring," agreed the man.

"Stop smirking!" rapped the woman. "*Our* time is still six months away. But for you, my dear John, the sands have already run out."

The girl continued her reverie. "We're all pretty ultimate, aren't we? I didn't give him much of a chance, you know. It's really pretty much like shooting a sitting bird. Seducing a man of his age. Just as I was beginning to develop an affection for him, he sells me to you. He trades my body, in order to gratify his own overwhelming lust."

The woman was indignant. "I resent the suggestion that I have deceived anybody. I made a bargain and I kept faithfully to it."

"A bargain to seduce an apparently innocent girl."

"I am discussing the issue of *deception,* not the morality of sex. In any case, *you* were a party to the seduction of this apparently innocent girl."

"I didn't suggest it."

"No, but you jumped at the chance, didn't you?"

"Yes, I admit I jumped at the chance. I'd jump again."

"Is that intended as a compliment?"

"Yes, it is."

The woman stopped the rapid-fire barrage and said slowly and pointedly, "Perhaps we should return to your academic friends, Professor. What exactly are you going to tell them?"

"I shall insist on a thorough investigation of the whole thing."

"Would that be wise? Is there anything in this business that would profit from thorough investigation? How you purloined my diary in order to discover my condition on a certain day of the month? Would that make a favorable headline in the daily press, do you think?"

"I suppose it will give you great satisfaction to see me chucked out—wasn't that the way you put it?"

"It will give me no satisfaction at all. Quite the contrary. You are not going to be chucked out, for the good and sufficient reason that we—Cynthia and I—have need of financial support."

"What the hell do you mean by that?"

"Simply this. You will sign a statement admitting the paternity of Cynthia's child. The statement will never be produced so long as your income is properly diverted to us, to Cynthia and me. And by your income, my dear John, I do not mean your academic salary. I also mean all the profitable little side lines. I mean your income as your accountant sees it."

"Well, of all the bitches in creation, you're just about the last!"

The woman smiled at the girl. "Didn't I say I'd make him suffer?"

"What am I supposed to live on?" asked the man in furious indignation.

"Naturally you will live here with us. What else?"

"Think of the scandal, woman."

"Scandal, yes. Scandal most horrible. But since it cannot be proved that Cynthia's child is your child, the university will take no steps. You said so yourself."

"But, good God, do you think I'm going to slave my guts out for a couple of women like you, together all the time, together and laughing in my face? I'll clear out once and for all if you push me too far. I'm warning you, Helen."

"Rubbish, hysterical nonsense. A few minutes ago you admitted to waiting ten years to make me—actually it was twelve years. If you tried to run away, I could bring you back, just by raising my little finger—like that!"

The woman held up a fist, but with the fifth finger extended. The man pondered the implications of this remark. Then he burst out again, "I'm not going to have the two of you going off. . . ."

"Off to bed, is that what you mean? Leaving you to your own little solitary. What other prospect is there, my poor John, unless Cynthia or I should take pity on you? You see, with women like us, there is only one difficult problem, children. Happily, you have provided for us in this regard, just as you are going to provide for us financially speaking. Happily also, you will be able to help with the children, to wash them when they stagger about the house with appallingly dirty hands, the little dears you have imposed on us with such biological ferocity."

The woman smiled from the couch on both the man and the girl. "Now, with all this unpleasantness settled and concluded, how shall we proceed to amuse ourselves? I believe television is offering one of its more popular domestic dramas."

The author's fingers were streaked with ink as he came to the end of his crass little story. He read it through from the beginning, a satisfied smile on his face. Coming along nicely, he thought to himself, although two of the characters, the man and the girl, still needed development. He'd better say what the man was a professor of. Best to choose something in the sciences, so as to put things on the right side of the two cultures.

The author left his desk to make himself a cup of coffee. While waiting for the kettle, it struck him like a thunderclap. He hit his forehead with the palm of his hand, symbolically in the classical theatrical gesture. Obviously, oh, so obviously, this must be a play, not a story. How much easier to strengthen the professor on the stage, to strengthen him into a formidable bullish creature, merely stage business. He could lengthen out the initial dinner party. He'd have it strange and obscure, with a lot of oblique remarks. All the girl need do, right through, would be to look mysterious. The older woman would carry the show quite easily. He'd already got her well in hand. At the beginning he'd mislead everybody into thinking it was the usual triangle problem, with the man and woman married and with the man just on the point of running off with the young bit of stuff. He could keep it going this way right up to the end of the first act. How about bringing down the curtain by letting it out that *both* women were pregnant? A good dramatic punch, that. It would mislead an audience into thinking the play turned on the dilemma of whether the man could leave his wife, now she was pregnant.

In the second act he'd pull out all the stops, twisting things in a way nobody expected. My God, what a story it was, when he came to think about it dispassionately. Two Lesbians, both pregnant by the same man, with the delicious idea of one of them trading herself to him in order to get at the other. It had never been thought of before, not even by the great men, not even by Boccaccio, so far as he could remember, let alone by the ordinary run of modern writers. It was brilliant, even if he said it only to himself. Another thing, wasn't it superb the way he needed only three characters? It should be possible for any theater to afford the hundred-and-fifty-a-week class. This would take a lot of the strain off, because actors and actresses in that class can make bricks out of straw, not that there need be much straw in this thing. It couldn't miss, not with the sex craze in the theater running so strongly. He could see it just running and running, maybe five years?

In a fine frenzy, the author rushed back to his desk. On a new pad he began rapidly to sketch in the opening of his first act. It never occurred to him that his characters supplied a subconscious need for something to dominate. The writer interested in plot follows the path of structure and order. The writer interested in the pathological aspects of humanity has rarely anything of logic or of structure. He is seeking to satisfy the basic human instinct to dominate, if not real flesh and blood, well, at least the figments of his own imagination.

CATTLE TRUCKS

Dionysus was the first to awaken. It hadn't been at all bad, the life of a god in ancient Greece. But when Rome took over, mere existence became a desperate bore. So the gods all retired to Olympus, to "sleep it out." It was hoped things would be better after a few millennia had slipped away.

Dionysus was all agog to take a quick first look around. He decided on a complete circumnavigation of the world. His flight took him across the great waters to the west of the Pillars of Hercules, to the continent now known as America. Here he gorged himself in astonishment.

One afternoon, in a place called California, he thought he would try out for himself one of the amazing little boxes, constructed, it seemed, from glass and metal, in which the mortals were now everlastingly scurrying around. He could see them below him, moving in almost continuous streams along a vast network of roads. From above, it all looked utterly aimless, like a big mound of ants. But there must be something to it, to all this commotion, Dionysus supposed.

The god slid unobtrusively into the first empty automobile he could find. To make the thing move demanded more ingenuity than he had expected. When at last he had the trick of it, he drove at a moderate pace onto a nearby highway. He soon mastered the standard practice of directing the box between two of the lines marked on the road. So what? He couldn't imagine why anybody, even a mortal, would want to behave in this fashion. He felt there had to be more zip in it somewhere. He must be missing something. But the best he could find to do was to press the pedal harder and harder, the pedal that made the box go faster and faster. Even so, it was tame stuff.

There came a great whining noise. In fact, the noise gave Dionysus quite an ungodlike start. It issued apparently from another moving box, one that had suddenly come up close behind. On top of this other box a red light flashed unceasingly. Howling like Cerberus, the watchdog of Hades, the box went past him and then began to slow down. So Dionysus in turn went past the flashing box, which then immediately picked up speed. It seemed the other box was intent on playing some kind of game, a strange game, it was true. Dionysus wondered if his box should also be displaying a flashing light and if there was some way in which it could be made to howl in this outrageous manner. A dozen times or more he went past the thing, his foot stamped flat on the pedal, the one that made his box go faster. Then the other box began to crowd him to the roadside. He thought about giving it a knock which would send it in a great arc through the air. Then he thought there might be some interest in stopping, to find out what it was that could howl so long and so loud.

Unfortunately, just when he expected to get to the bottom

of the business, the howling stopped, although the light went on flashing. Dionysus saw a man coming toward him and felt an intense wonderment. The man was wearing a huge hat, there were black patches over his eyes—to shield them from the Sun, it seemed—and his gait would have befitted the god of Insolence. "You aiming to fly?"

"Yes, I am intending to fly."

"Well, you're doing no more flying today. See here, Charlie, I'm arresting you right now. You can fly after you've talked to the judge. Your license, Mac."

"License?"

"You're going to get the book, sweetie, oh, how you're going to get the book. Maybe you've got a name?"

"Dionysus."

"Dionysus what?"

"Dionysus nothing."

"Okay, Dionysus Q. Squirt, you're coming with me. We'll straighten out the car and the license afterward. Come on, Mr. Wise Guy, make it snappy."

As Dionysus climbed from the car, the cop put a hand over his gun. The god had previously adjusted his height to fit the car. Now he adjusted it to fit this new situation. He stood a head taller than the cop. With a swoop, faster than lightning, he picked the man up, swung him over the front of the box, and fastened him securely there. Then he drove back onto the highway, leaving the prowl car with its flashing light abandoned by the roadside.

An hour later Dionysus found himself approaching a large airport. The road took him right into it. The many people thronging Los Angeles Airport were intrigued by the big man with a curly golden beard who walked majestically into one of the airline buildings, leaving his car triple-parked outside. They were intrigued by the big buck deer strapped across its front. The deer turned out to be alive. Unwisely, three porters released the animal, whereupon it raced after the bearded man, emitting a bellow that sounded uncannily like "Hi, Mac." As the prancing deer spread the utmost confusion, everybody looked for the strange hunter with the golden beard, but Dionysus had slipped invisibly onto a plane just taking off for New York.

Once inside the plane, Dionysus became visible again. Nobody took any particular notice as he moved into an empty seat. A tinny, glutinous sound was coming from some place immediately above his head. Music he supposed it was, but of an utterly commonplace quality, so commonplace as to be scarcely credible. It was his first experience of actual physical nausea, for in the ordinary way of things gods are never sick. These appalling sounds made him feel as if he were going to throw up.

Mercifully, the music stopped once the plane had lifted off the ground, once, miraculously, they were flying. Mortals were flying, ordinary mortals. Dionysus thought he had never seen so many ordinary mortals. They were packed together like cattle, five in a row, row after row of the creatures. The mere sight of them all, sitting there like so many huge pumpkins, depressed him. He considered how things might be livened up a bit. He tried singing in a tremendous bass voice, but nobody noticed it. They were all staring at little flickering pictures, their ears plugged solid with some device or other. Dionysus tried it himself. He heard more music, this time distantly projected against the roar of the plane. It had the quality of a sludge pump.

Without warning, there was a harsh crackle above his head. A disembodied voice began, "Well, folks, this is your captain." The volume was enormous, almost sufficient to shatter his eardrums. The voice went on to advise them to look out of the plane on the right-hand side. Dionysus gathered from the announcement that something quite stupendous was to be seen, so he tried to look out just as the captain had advised. He found the window so small that almost nothing was visible.

The plane gave a little shake, a kind of shrug, like an animal settling itself more comfortably. A notice flashed up in front of the god's nose: FASTEN YOUR SEAT BELT.

One of the stewardesses paraded up and down the aisle, checking the instant obedience of the passengers. By now the plane had resumed its smooth ride.

"I want to go to the john," a woman complained.

"Not while the seat-belt sign is on, please," was the firm command. The stewardess came abreast of the god. She was a pretty little thing, trim and wiry, hardworking, but reduced by the system to a prissy schoolmarm. She pointed imperiously at the god's midriff. "Fasten your belt. Your belt, please."

Dionysus rose from his seat. He took hold of the girl and marched her back along the aisle to a little cubicle, a place where coats were normally kept. The girl protested loudly, but nobody heard. Individual T.V. had the whole planeload in thrall. The stewardess was astonished to find the cubicle no longer small. It had suddenly become amply large enough for the god's purpose. The stewardess shrieked and fought, but the fuss was of no avail. Off came the uniform, off came the standardized starched shirt. The shrieks changed to laughter as wave after wave of tingling and wingling swept over the girl. She emerged from the cubicle ten minutes later, her face flushed and her eyes shining. Nobody noticed the change except the second stewardess. A frenzied whispered conversation between the girls made it clear to Dionysus that more of the same was needed. The second girl also proved quite defenseless against the jingling and wingling. She too soon emerged wide-eyed from the cubicle.

Thereafter both girls giggled and laughed as they walked the plane. Time came for lunch. Now, if there is one thing your airline stewardess comes to hate with a furious intensity, it is the serving of appalling trays of appalling food. The operation has a certain similarity to the stuffing of turkeys, except turkeys demand more or less decent food, not the precooked, overcooked slush that passes for the usual airline meal. Your stewardess comes to hate all those little packages, packages for salt, pepper, butter, packages for package people on a package flight.

The girls were having none of it this time. The whole lot was thrown in together. No cocktails were served. Instead, all the alcohol went in, along with the meat, the potatoes, the dessert, and the cheese. They served the mixture in big pudding bowls.

Nobody noticed the difference, except a man traveling in solitary splendor in the first-class section. He angrily demanded to know what the white stuff was on top. The stewardess gave a deep, bell-like laugh. "Crabmeat garnish, sir." The man became still more furiously angry. He revealed his exalted identity–president, he was, of the airline itself. Instantly, the wrath of Dionysus descended without pity. Struck dumb in midsentence, the fellow collapsed into his seat, his eyes riveted forever on individual T.V. Never again would this particular monster be permitted to manipulate people.

Dionysus started to sing again. This time he was joined by the two girls and by five of the passengers. Such was the measure of his success, seven from a total of one hundred or more. These seven were now rescued from a kind of living death. The rest were too far gone, too far below the surface, they had become bond-slaves to the god of Inanition. They sat there congealed, ears stuffed up, eyes stuffed up, brains stuffed up, all semblance of intellect completely dissolved away.

The plane landed. The stewardesses busied themselves. There were none of the usual glassy smiles, just genuine laughter. One of them chuckled as she announced, "On behalf of the crew, I'd like to say how very much we've enjoyed having you with us today, and with what pleasure we look forward to having you with us again, in the nearest future."

The girls smiled with intense warmth as the man with the golden beard strode away into the airline building. Once the passengers were all gone, both girls raced down the plane, back to the cubicle. It really was very small, really *too* small, they both thought rather sadly.

Dionysus reached the main concourse. He heard a voice saying, "Will Mrs. Finkelstein and Mr. Fink please report. . . ." Then the terrible music started again. It was the same abomination as before. It made him sick in the same way, churning his stomach over. With a tremendous concentration of will, he conquered the nausea. The music stopped. Everybody in the concourse braced themselves for a further announcement concerning Mrs. Finkelstein and Mr. Fink. But no further sound seemed to come from the speakers.

It wasn't that Dionysus had interfered with the electrical feeder lines to the speakers. He was absorbing all the sound. The music was still really coming through, but Dionysus was taking it all for himself, leaving nothing to be heard by the milling throng of people in the concourse. He took the music, every note of it, for a long time, all deep into his belly. As one glutinous note after another went inside him, it seemed to Dionysus as if he were being pumped up and up to the size of an enormous gasbag. There was a limit to what even he could do, to what any god could do. At last the limit was reached, not another single note could he manage to pack inside himself. Dionysus let the whole lot go, in a colossal burp that shook the concourse like a thunderclap. Windows were shattered, cracks appearing everywhere in walls and ceiling. People raced for the exits, convinced that planes were exploding to the left and to the right on the runways outside.

Dionysus surveyed the wreckage and smiled to himself as he stepped through a gap in the outer wall. The evening air was warm and clear, just right for a return to Olympus. He knew what he was going to do when he got home–sleep. He also knew something else. Very definitely, he was flying the rest of his journey on foot.

WELCOME TO SLIPPAGE CITY

It's amazing how many people have a good idea and then foul it up. Take the theologians. When they thought up the Devil they were dead-set on the right track, but then they go off with a ridiculous notion. Imagine the Devil bothering with souls one by one, dealing with you or me on an individual basis, like a common tinker. The critical thing to remember is that the Devil thinks big, reaping his harvests by the million, like he did in the case of Slippage City.

Suppose you wanted to start up a hell of a city. You'd probably put it in a lousy climate. Well, the Devil didn't make that mistake. He put his City in a beautiful place, a place with a wonderful climate. There was a plain about fifty miles wide between a chain of mountains and the sea. It was a place of nearly perpetual sunshine. Yet it was no desert, quite the reverse. What happened was that every day the air moved in and out over the sea. It came in saturated with moisture during the early morning. There was always a heavy dew with a light mist. The water soaked into the fertile ground before the sun climbed high in the sky. Then, in the heat of the day, the air began to move seaward. It was now so warmed by the sun that it took a big charge of water vapor from the sea, ready to be delivered again to the land on the morrow. Because the air was always dry in the evening, the land cooled off rapidly during the night. The nights were never hot or clammy–in fact, it was mostly necessary to sleep under a couple of blankets.

The City itself became established near the sea, toward the northern end of the plain. Here was a multitude of little hills and valleys, verdant and bird-filled. The houses of the first settlers fitted tastefully into the landscape. Ample water for the first modest needs could be piped from the mountains, or even pumped from simple wells. Crops grew abundantly in the plain, aided by the beginnings of irrigation. Because the people had no thought of profit, the food they grew was real food. The vegetables tasted like real vegetables, the fruit like real fruit, not the flashy, spray-soaked rubbish that would come a hundred years later with the ultimate transmogrification of the City. The children grew up brown and strong. There seemed an infinity of hills and valleys to be explored on horseback. At that early time, the simplest folk possessed horses, just as naturally as they possessed clothing and shelter. Later, with the march of "progress," only the children of the very rich would be able to afford horses. Later, not even the children of the very rich would have space to play in, the apparent infinity would turn out to be no infinity at all.

But the City grew only slowly in the beginning, because a great desert on the far side of the mountains separated it from all large centers of population. It was a long, hazardous journey to reach the City, so immigrants came at first only in a tiny trickle. The immigrants brought labor, craftsmanship, and knowledge. In most ways they gave as much to the City as they took from it. The fields became trimmer, the buildings more substantial, the initial crudities of life were smoothed away. The City became widely known for its beauty, yet because of the remoteness it grew only slowly.

At last came transportation, first the railroad. Yet the immediate effects of making access to the City much less arduous than before were more preparatory than dramatic. It was the same thing as before, but *a poco a poco*. More immigrants, more development, more prosperity. The railway permitted exports, at first mostly fruit, which at this stage was still of excellent quality. Orange groves were now to be found everywhere throughout the fertile strip of land, stretching back from the sea by the full fifty miles in some places. Prosperity and the amenities of life became added to the natural beauty of the City. Everybody who lived there was entirely convinced of the City's preeminence as a desirable place to live. This conviction they passed on to their children, so a mystique concerning the City became firmly established. Wealthy folk came from great distances to live there. Spacious homes were built. The way of life was leisurely, almost casual, at this stage.

Great, far-off industrial centers took note of the City's "potential." It was a most pleasant place for successful executives to live in. It would be possible for well-paid executives to live cheek by jowl with the wealthy, for them to build similar homes, for them to share in the social life of the City, even for them to marry into the families of the truly wealthy. Industrial buildings could be erected more cheaply than elsewhere, in spite of the remoteness of the City, because the equable, all round the year, climate demanded very little in the way of tough, solid construction. Some industrial activities could indeed be carried on with advantage in the open air, without any buildings at all. So industry began to move in, at first in a small way of course, then *poco più mosso*. It was while industrial development was thus in its early acceleration that extensive oil deposits were discovered in the vicinity of the City.

Here was the first one of the Devil's jokers slipped into the pack.

A forest of derricks soon appeared on what used to be a beautiful beach. For the first time an amenity of the City had been destroyed.

Great riches fell suddenly and unexpectedly into the lap of those who happened to own the oil-bearing land. These riches became the envy of other members of the community. The concept of the desirability of "wealth" had now become firmly established. The concept had first been imported with the rich people from outside, then emphasized by the industrialists from outside. Among the new seekers after wealth were the "real estate men." So far, dealings in property had consisted in the straightforward buying and selling of houses of quality. It was realized now by the real estate men that an ever-increasing flow of immigrants would eventually yield great profits to those with the cunning to buy more and more of the extensive open areas around the City. These could be "developed," as the term had it.

Water was an obvious problem. The natural daily air movement back and forth between land and sea was quite insufficient to provide for a vast increase in the population of the City. Water was therefore taken from the surrounding mountains, water was pumped across the desert from distant rivers. Outlying communities lost their water and their lands became scrub. Once-green mountain valleys became sand-blown.

There is an old story of a man who chanced to save the life of a king. The king invited his rescuer to demand any reward he should please, expecting, no doubt, that one of his many daughters would be asked for. But no, the man took a chessboard with its sixty-four squares, saying he wanted a single grain of wheat for the first square, two grains for the second square, four for the third and so on until the sixty-fourth square was reached. The king, somewhat disappointed, begged that some other, some worthier, gift be considered. But his savior would have no other. Reluctantly, the king ordered the keeper of his household to make the necessary computation and to provide what was asked for. To his astonishment, it was reported back to him that the royal granary did not contain the appropriate quantity of wheat nor, in the view of the keeper of the household, was so much wheat to be found in the whole world.

There's nothing more here than the Devil's hoariest old trick, this simple two-by-two multiplication. Humans fall for it every time. Get humans started on something they like, then bring in the two-by-two business, that's the standard formula. The result must always be disaster because the multiplication can't go on indefinitely, it must blow up in your face. Give a kid a piece of candy to suck to keep him quiet. The kid naturally becomes conditioned to liking candy. He buys two pieces of it as soon as he receives his Saturday penny. Then he buys four when he lands his first job, then eight with the first pay increase, and so on. Result, teeth drop out. Or one drink, two drinks, four drinks. . . .

In just this simple way all really big human disasters are engineered. So it was with the City. The flow of immigrants had increased like the wheat grains on the chessboard, two by two, *a poco a poco,* for a century or more. At first it was just the ones and twos and fours. Nobody minded the immigrants then, they were good for the City, it was said. Quite suddenly, with the development of the automobile and the airplane, the thing blew up, the flow burst into a raging torrent. Human kind came to the City at a rate of one thousand a day. They came in automobiles across the desert. They came in airplanes from the far corners of the Earth. Like the keeper of the household, compute it out, and you will find it amounts to one third of a million throbbing souls a year, three million or more to a decade.

The real estate developers made their clean-up. They carved the land into tiny lots. On each tiny lot they put a shoddy little home built from lath and chicken wire. Everywhere the developers delved and rooted, pushing their snouts further and further into the remote nooks and crannies of the City's hilly environment. They became very wealthy, these developers. They bought massive earth-moving machinery and they bulldozed the terrain to whatever shape or pattern suited their swelling purses. Gone now were homes set tastefully into natural surroundings. This was the era of ugly little boxes, set apart at microscopic distances, scarring the countryside, everywhere, in every available open space.

There was a big vocal group in the City, representing newspaper interests, interests in radio and T.V. The group existed with the aim of creating "needs." With an utterly wearying insistence, they dinned it into people's minds that everybody "needed" this particular article or that particular article. The less an article was really required, the more insistent was the vocal group. Their motto consisted of a single word, "progress." They looked with cooperative disfavor on the few persons they deemed to be obstructors of progress. There were still a few of these in the City, there were farmers who had the simple desire to go on doing what their fathers and grandfathers had done, to grow oranges and lemons. These farmers owned blocks of land which offered the prospect of further "clean-ups" to the developers. So the farmers were frozen out, like this. Now the City had become so prosperous, it was necessary to raise enormous taxes. A land tax was introduced, a tax which it was utterly beyond the farmer's competence to pay—the whole return on his crop did not come near to equaling these savage taxes. So, perforce, the farmer had to sell, there was no alternative. Like a spreading plague, "development" bulldozed the orchards everywhere over the City. The urbanization was at last complete. The sprawling complex measured some fifty miles across, some two thousand square miles, mainly covered with rabbit hutches. Some of the older, pleasant houses remained, it is true, and it was in these the oil men, the industrialists, the developers, and those who had become wealthy through merely being vocal, lived.

Because of the naturally uneven terrain, because of the size of the City, because of the manner of its growth, transport could not be organized in any straightforward, or even rational, way. Because of the great demand for homes, men would often live thirty miles from their place of employment, particularly if they felt themselves "lucky" in their present home. Because of the generally scattered nature of the City, it was common for close friends to live in widely separated places. These factors forced a system of transportation the like of which had not been seen on the Earth before. Wide highways were driven through the very heart of the City, not just one highway, but an intricate complex linking the sprawling communities of the whole urban area. These were highways of rapid access. They were crowded with furious, fast-moving vehicles throughout all daylight hours and through most of the night, too. Everybody in the City acquired the habit of driving everywhere by car. The leg muscles of the people atrophied, and this became a cause of the early deaths that were soon to sweep the City.

The City, of all the cities of the Earth, was perhaps the least suited to the use of the automobile as a primary means of transport. The very air movement, in and out over the sea, which had led to the founding of the City, was now a terrible liability. The air became a stagnant pool into which the by-products of the incomplete combustion of oil gradually accumulated. The strong sunlight induced chemical reactions, resulting in a kind of tear gas. Half a dozen times in a day the eyes of the people would burst into uncontrollable fits of weeping, as they vainly sought to wash themselves clean of the smear of chemicals that latched continuously onto the front surfaces of the eyeballs. It was difficult now for anything except humans to live in this appalling atmospheric sewer. The oranges that grew on the few remaining trees reacted sharply to changed circumstances by suddenly becoming very small and sour to the taste.

The city at this stage was much the most restless place to be found anywhere, but instead of this being thought a disadvantage, it was extolled as a virtue. People shuffled into their cars on weekends and drove hither and thither quite aimlessly. They weren't going anywhere, they were just going. They drove to the sea and were disappointed they couldn't keep on, lemming-like, on and on over the ocean.

Sensitive people began to crack up. Mental hospitals became overfull. Sometimes the crack-up took a form which reacted seriously on the City itself. There was a sprinkling of deliberate arsonists, pitiful people so desperately needing attention from their fellowmen that they were led to seek it in any way whatsoever, if necessary by lighting fires on the tinder-dry mountain slopes fringing the City. All the surrounding natural vegetation was steadily burned away. Often the fires got quite out of hand. They would extend blazing fingers into the outer boundaries of the City, destroying the homes of those who had sought to avoid the noise and racket of its central regions.

The City was not exactly without rain. Rain fell only very occasionally, but when it did so the heavens burst apart and several inches would fall within a few hours. Three inches falling everywhere over two thousand square miles amounts to several hundred million tons of water. This vast torrent had to sweep directly through the City in order to reach the sea. It was not unknown for people to be drowned in the very streets, so great could be the flood. With the surrounding hillsides burned clear of the covering of natural vegetation, soil was carried down in huge quantities by these occasional floods. Shoots of mud poured relentlessly onto the confines of the City, often overwhelming houses that had survived the fires themselves. Where houses of lath and chicken wire had been built on the foothills, it was common for the floods to produce an actual dislodgment of the foundations, slippage, it was called.

The imposition of physical distress is only a minor aspect of the Devil's activities, another bad error of the medieval theologian. The Devil is much more concerned with the induction of psychological distress. This thrilling, throbbing City of three million people provided the Devil with opportunities more varied and more rich than one could ever hope to describe in close detail.

The City was financially prosperous. It offered a rich return to anybody willing to work really hard, anybody of reasonable intelligence and competence. Acquisition of money was now the chief symbol of success among its people. The temptations were strong. In exchange for money, "services" of all kinds were offered on a scale unknown anywhere else on Earth. The people felt the "need" to acquire a never-ending stream of gadgets, so well had the vocal group done its work. Women were attracted by men who succeeded in amassing fortunes. In sum, the men were impelled to seek after money throughout the major part of their waking hours. It was really just the two-by-two multiplication all over again. Work spells gain, gain spells demand, demand spells work, round and round in an amplifying cycle. The amplification blew up, of course, as it had to do. It blew up through the men working themselves into early graves. The endless overwork under artificial conditions without natural exercise killed the men in their fifties, sometimes in their forties. Even this macabre situation was converted to profitability by the gravediggers. The most successful gravediggers were among the wealthiest of the citizens and they contributed handsomely to the City's enterprises.

The men were so much "at work," as the years passed, that they saw progressively less of their wives. The wives became more and more engrossed in their children. The upbringing of children was a depressing affair in itself, however, since there was no proper place in the vicinity of the home where children might get together and play. This was true even for the very wealthy, who made shift by sending their kids to expensive holiday camps, but even this was no substitute for simply being able to slip "out" and play at any moment of the day. The children grew up bored and restless, veritable pests to have around the house. On weekends they could be taken to the sea or to the mountains, but with everyone else also taking their children to the sea or to the mountains, the roads were a nightmare, and the beaches and mountains were ridiculously overcrowded.

These weekend trips were a disguised trap. Because everybody else was doing the same thing, there was a sense of "togetherness" about it all. Because everybody else was doing it, it had to be the right way to live. These weekend trips disguised the fates now overtaking the several members of the family. For the husband, working himself to the scrap heap. For the children, leaving home in a vain attempt to escape insupportable boredom. For the wife, something still worse.

As he grows older, the natural impulse of man is to prove to himself that he is not growing older. This he will attempt to do in a fashion depending very much on the conventions of the community in which he happens to live. In Slippage City, men did it by attempting to attract sexually some younger woman or girl. There was nothing which did more for a man—as he moved into his forties—than to find himself climbing into bed with a woman of twenty. Thereby did he prove his vigor, at any rate to his own satisfaction, if not to that of an impartial commentator. You see, there were other circumstances, quite apart from vigor, working powerfully on his side. Girls were strongly encouraged in the City to do well for themselves financially. Since men in their forties were more likely, statistically speaking, to be wealthy than those in their twenties, it was only natural for the moderately aging to prove popular with the better-favored girls. Overcome with his triumph, heady with sexual nectar, it was common for the successful middle-aged man to sever the bonds of matrimony. The phrase "until death us do part" came to have little influence or meaning. Who was going to die, anyway?

So it was common for women in their late thirties or early forties to find themselves suddenly abandoned both by husband and children, for this was the time when the children were avid to leave home. It was too late, almost, to begin again. Life itself had blown up in their faces. To compound the tragedy, "friends" dropped away too, for married women did not welcome the divorcée into their homes, especially when divorcée and husband had known each other these many years past. Such women, then, were obliged to keep company with others in a similar plight. A few succeeded in fighting back, but the majority fell just where they were intended to fall by the Devil, who had planned it all so long ago.

Ironically, just when it seemed as if there would be no limit to his success, the Devil overreached himself. Ironically, too, it was the intervention of a simple, innocent girl that brought about his downfall.

Polly Warburg was one of those who crossed the desert by car, descending into Slippage City through a pass in the fringing mountains. She came with only a few possessions, only a little money, a pretty face, pitifully seeking her fortune. Another girl, some years older, from the same hometown, had done very well for herself, it was rumored. Polly could have done all right back in the hometown, but it would have been hopelessly dull. Here it was all glitter and "life."

The girl innocently and optimistically tried to break into one of the more glamorous, highly paid activities. She was rapidly and effectively disillusioned. Rather desperate now, Polly searched around for some humbler occupation. It soon boiled down to a choice between the life of a night-club cutie, with a big, blue butterfly on her backside, and a job in one of the new superplus hotels. The nature of the second job wasn't specified, suspicious in itself. The man who interviewed her said it was a daytime job, so Polly in her innocence thought it must be on the level. As it happened, the job was in fact a more or less proper one. It wasn't really a job at all, or more accurately, it shouldn't have been a job at all. Lots of things go wrong in superplus hotels. The plumbing doesn't quite work. Noise somehow gets piped up from the street, presumably through the steel structure, so the nineteenth floor is noisier than the street itself. Your room gets stuffy and you can't find any heating control and the windows won't open. There is no end to your troubles in such places. Most people accept the all-pervasive inconvenience as a part of the deal, because it is not usual for most people to stay in superplus hotels. Not so your experienced traveler, your up-and-on-top executive. They holler like hell for the manager. Something has to be done about it, make no mistake. Now the simplest thing to do, so say the psychologists, is to let the manager be out of town and to substitute a pretty face in his stead. Let the girl smile, let her hear the complaint, let her note it down, and let absolutely nothing to be done about it. To the delight of the rogues who run these abominable places, the method works, particularly when the pretty face can be combined with a sweet temperament. Polly had both these assets and that was why she walked immediately into a job which many girls would have been glad to have.

Of course, it never occurred to Polly that she was a mere face, a front-woman sheltering an inefficient, greedy organization. She hadn't been in the City long enough for its influence to have penetrated very far. She was living in its superficialities, like the bright lights at night and the sea and the mountains on weekends. She was adequately paid and she was always meeting important people, admittedly under rather trying circumstances, but one day it might lead to something, she persuaded herself. In short, Polly was happy. This in itself was an asset, since even happiness had commercial value in Slippage City.

One morning Polly was walking through the reception lobby when she saw two chubby men coming down from the mezzanine floor. They were wearing gay straw hats and there were big, fire-brick-red rosettes in the buttonholes of their light linen coats. Polly supposed they were from the big convention which was holding its meetings on the mezzanine floor. She gave the two chubby men one of her warmest smiles and passed on. She left them still talking. Not in her wildest dreams could she have guessed about what.

Not only Polly, but the whole management believed the hotel to be "entertaining" the annual convention of broom-handle manufacturers. Actually, the hotel was doing nothing of the sort. It was entertaining a convention of Devils from outer space. They came from all the planets on which suffering and turmoil existed. They came to compare notes and to discuss ways and means. Their number was large, far more than would ever have gone into a convention hall, even a political convention, if–being Devils–they hadn't possessed mastery over space and time. Of the two on whom Polly had smiled, one was our own, workaday, terrestrial Devil. The other was the Devil from α Serpentis, none other than the Dean of all Devils.

The convention had been called by the terrestrial Devil precisely to demonstrate his new city, for Slippage City had originality, it had facets of devilry which he felt sure would be instructive to his interstellar colleagues. On the whole, the convention gave him a good hearing, but the Devil from α Serpentis was not convinced, and it was Serpens himself whom our terrestrial Devil wanted most to convince. The two of them had still been arguing the matter while they walked down the stairs from the mezzanine floor, they had been arguing as Polly had smiled on them.

"There, look at that," exclaimed Serpens. "That's a good-looker for you, and can you have her when you want her, will she come running at the snap of your fingers? Will she my fanny. Let me tell you, Earth, my boy, your system is a wash-out. That girl will get herself married. Someone else, not you, will work on her exactly the way he feels like working. Okay, so she'll be divorced, so what? She'll get married again, twice, three times, maybe. Then, at the end of it all, she's yours, spoiled goods. I like 'em young and fresh myself, same as vegetables."

At this the terrestrial Devil became a little angry. He could have one little girl for the taking, he pointed out, anytime he wanted. What his system did was to give quantity, hundreds of thousands, soon millions. The Devil from α Serp replied that, while he must acknowledge it to be largely a matter of taste, he himself preferred one tasty dish to a veritable mountain of indigestible stuff. Then he broke off the conversation in a rather pointed way and went over to chat with the Devil from β Orionis.

After this there was no other alternative, of course, but for the terrestrial Devil to give an open demonstration to the whole of his convention of all that could be done in Slippage City to a girl like Polly Warburg, in fact, to Polly Warburg herself. Wheels were made to revolve. Polly received a communication the following day from a glamour agency, one she had tried to interest in the first place. The offer from the agency was a distinctly good one, in fact, a really excellent one, as a thoroughly well-established independent agent confirmed to her.

Polly was naturally elated to find her talents so worthily, if tardily, recognized. Her agent pointed out a possible hitch in the fine print attached to the contract which Polly signed, to the effect that the agreement would become null and void should a certain wealthy backer of the glamour project withdraw his support. The clause was quite a normal one, the agent said, not to worry about it.

The following day the rather attractive young man who was handling the matter "from the other side" told Polly, in the strictest confidence, that he saw no prospect of support being withdrawn if she could see her way to affording the wealthy backer a few slight favors, in fact, a weekend of slight favors. The backer, he said, was a splendid, jolly fellow, generous and openhanded, humorous and gay, indeed, a girl could do worse.

Polly, in her innocence, had been deceived before, but always by verbal promises, never after an actual contract had been signed. She was now of a divided mind. In the past she had given of her person without receiving the promised reward. Was it sensible to stint a wealthy backer who surely must produce a real reward? On the other hand, once bitten, twice shy. Polly was suspicious now about all men and their motives. In a divided mind, she went to see the older girl, the girl from her hometown. The older girl told her the people she was dealing with had a "good name in the business." As for the wealthy backer, what of it? Wasn't it done every day? She'd be a little fool to pass up such an opportunity.

So it came about that Polly agreed to meet her backer, for a weekend's assignment at a pleasant house on the best of the City's beaches.

The Devil, our own terrestrial Devil, turned up for the assignment in a well-groomed condition. He turned up in human shape, for there was no point in frightening the girl out of her wits, not right at the beginning. For the first hour or so Polly was nervous, but the Devil's conversation was so well judged to the level of her intellect that soon she felt quite at her ease. She didn't like to drink too much in the circumstances, of course. When the Devil pressed her in a jocular way, she accepted "a small one." In volume it may have been small. In impact it had a mule's kick.

The Devil then went about his business with a characteristic skill and efficiency. In a flash he had the clothes off the girl, burned to a cinder, they were, and without harming the girl. She giggled as he tumbled her into bed. She giggled louder and louder as the affair prospered. Indeed, it suddenly occurred to the Devil how very very warm this girl was, temperature-wise. Her nether quarters were heating up far too much for his liking. It was all a little like the outburst of some enormous star, a supernova, up to fantastic temperatures in the twinkling of an eye. The girl had him now in an iron grip, just where he could least afford an iron grip. Too late, the Devil realized he'd been tricked. It had all been done in the drink, the replacement of Polly Warburg by this ultraviolet-hot she-bitch. He knew exactly who had planned it, α Serp, of course, the Dean of Devils.

There was just time for the Devil to regret bitterly his decision to come in human shape before the thing went beyond all bounds. With the shriek of a tornado, he broke the iron grip. His momentum took him out through the house window. To cool off a bit, he drove himself like a mighty blast through the air, his lower quarters aglow like the jet of a rocket. Hollering and screaming, he careered like a jumping firecracker over the thronged streets and boulevards of the city of his creation. People looked up in wonderment, thinking there was no telling where progress would lead to next.

Polly Warburg saw nothing of all this, the real Polly, for she awoke only some hours later, to find herself sleeping in the old bed in the old house in the old hometown. She had no memory of what had happened in Slippage City. Nor was she aware that they'd better like it hot, the folks on α Serpentis.

THE AX

The weather was good, the skies clear, the air temperature not too high for uphill walking. A party of four young people, two men and two girls, approached the top of the mountain. The summit cairn was already tenanted by a brown-faced man, who seemed almost infinitely old to those young people. They passed the time of day, and the brown-faced man made the obvious joke about getting himself a lady companion. Then he set off down the gently sloping northern side, leaving the young people to laugh at a still better joke–the ice ax dangling across his back. Was the old boy really expecting snow in the middle of the summer?

Soon the young people were running down the same northern side of the mountain. It was good going, so they made a fast pace, gaining ground on the old man. Five hundred feet down from the summit, a subsidiary, twisting rocky ridge branched off to the right. It led down through the northern cliffs to the floor of the magnificent corrie below. It was not a difficult route by real climbing standards, but it needed constant care. The young people, as they charged down the more gentle upper slopes, were surprised to see the old man turn off the easier main ridge onto the subsidiary ridge. This was the route they intended to take themselves.

The brown-faced man was not more than a hundred feet below them when they started down the first broken rocks. They expected to catch him very quickly, but this was not what happened. Steadily, the gap between the solitary man and the twenty-year-olds opened up. The rougher the descent, the more the old man went ahead. He was using the ice ax skillfully, using it to save his legs from the jarring of the multitude of awkward downward steps. Year by year the legs accumulate small, irreparable damage to ligaments and cartilage, damage which the body cannot repair. Old legs, like old trees, carry the total debit of accidental damage taken over a whole lifetime. With the aid of his ax, the old man had learned to overcome something of this inevitable handicap, giving his superb natural balance an opportunity to show itself. An observer would have seen four healthy youngsters letting themselves carefully down little rock walls, down bits of scree and steep grass. He would also have seen the old man forging ahead of them, moving smoothly and gracefully, apparently without haste, in the style of the true mountaineer.

The youngsters didn't laugh at the sight of the ax when they came for a second time on the brown-faced man. He was sitting beside the lochan that nestled in the floor of the corrie. He'd been sitting there for perhaps twenty minutes, watching them, munching bits of chocolate mixed together with an apple. He offered them some of the chocolate and they were not embarrassed to accept it, as they would have been if he had offered it at the cairn at the top. Then they were off along the path at a good clip, anxious to do the six miles back to the nearest village before the shops closed for the day.

The old man stayed on long after the young people had gone. He sat in the afternoon sunshine, not because he was tired, but because he was in no hurry. It was a curious thing, as he had grown older he had got less tired, not more tired. Tweaks and twinges, yes, tired legs, no. The last time he had felt really tired was so far back in the past that he couldn't even bring it to mind. Where age showed itself, he thought wryly, was in his attitude to discomfort. He could face rain, wind, or blizzard with the same determination he'd always had, but *unnecessary* discomfort made him acutely miserable. It made him miserable to eat a bad dinner when he could get a good one, to sleep in an uncomfortable bed when a comfortable one was available, to stump ten miles along a hard road when he could ride in a car.

The ax was standing upright a few yards away, where he had stabbed it into soft ground. It was strong and light, beautifully made and, like himself, it was old. The ax had been given to him many years ago by an Italian mountaineer, a pioneer in South America. How many places had it stood as it was standing now? On first ascents in the Andes, on many an Alpine peak.

It was almost fifteen years since the day on the Obergabelhorn. With a guide, he had traversed the Weisshorn, descending the Schaligrat. The following day they had set out for the traverse of the Wellenkuppe and the Obergabelhorn. It was all perfectly straightforward. They had crossed the summit of the Wellenkuppe to the Great Gendarme. After the Gendarme they came to the steepening rocks of the Obergabelhorn itself. From here on, the climb was essentially on rock, so he had stopped to put the ax head safely into his rucksack–that was before rucksacks were made with special loops at the top and bottom for fastening an ax. The guide had been impatient with him for stopping. Couldn't he wedge the ax into the rucksack straps in the same way the guide himself had done? He had tried it, but during the climb there came a moment when he was forced to stoop and the ax had slipped out. It dropped on to an exceedingly steep snowslope flanking the ridge on which they were climbing. He had watched it slide with increasing speed, down toward the glacier thousands of feet below. Then it happened in a flash. The ax took a bounce, upended itself, and miraculously dug its point deep into a snowy ledge. There it stuck, standing upright, just as it was doing now.

He told the guide he was going down to retrieve it, but the guide said no, the slope was far too steep. They had argued, both determined men. To him, there was no question of leaving the ax. If it had gone down to the glacier, all very well. He would have written it off. But it hadn't. It had stopped. It was holding itself up, waiting to be fetched.

To the Swiss, this was a case of insanity. The route ahead to the summit of the Obergabelhorn was a rock climb, as also was the descent by the Arbengrat. An ax was almost superfluous from here on. Certainly there was no danger in going on. Equally certain, there *was* danger in attempting to retrieve the ax which his client had been fool enough to drop.

So they had argued, one in English, one in German, not able to understand each other very well. At last the Englishman had told the guide to fix his own price for the retrieval of the ax, but retrieved it was going to be, even if he had to go alone for it. This changed the situation, for a guide is paid to risk his life in his client's interest.

The guide had lowered the Englishman on a two-hundred-foot rope. Then the guide had climbed down to him in his steps, and they had again run out the rope. This brought him off the horribly steep part of the slope, to the ledges where the ax had fastened itself. With the ax, now, getting back to the ridge had not been impossibly difficult. Details of the rest of the traverse were almost lost from memory.

The guide had more than doubled his tariff for the day. The old man still remembered the two hundred francs he had paid over. A lot for an ax, but then it had been impossible to leave it, with its hand outstretched to him like that.

With a sigh, the brown-faced man got to his feet, slipped the ax through the special loop in his rucksack, and started down the track from the lochan to the lower valley.

AGENT 38

An agent's job is a lonely one. Agent Number 38 Zone 11 reflected so as he worked over his report for perhaps the twentieth time. He hadn't even a decent name to be known by. Just Number 38 of Zone 11, nothing more. It was irritating, degrading almost.

Reports of U.F.O.s (Unidentified Flying Objects) were of course commonplace, had been for twenty years. To allay public anxiety, an official inquiry had been necessary—that would be about ten years ago. The findings weren't too well received in some quarters. A lot of witnesses had been judged to be irresponsible publicity-seekers. Liars, in fact. And the more honest ones had been put down as victims of anxiety complexes. This had been Agent 38's own opinion at the time. A bunch of psychotic characters. How could objects whiz through the atmosphere, or whiz along outside the atmosphere, at the fantastic speeds that had been claimed? The accelerations would kill you in a moment.

According to the big boys, the way an anxiety complex works is this. You're all hotted up inside about something or other. You can't find any outlet for your bottled emotions in the real world. So you invent a phantom world. You force yourself to see things and hear things—U.F.O.s, in fact. In short, you go crazy.

Agent 38 could well believe he was suffering from an anxiety complex. Who wouldn't be after the troubles of the last few years? But how, in his case, could spotting a U.F.O. be of the slightest help to a bottled-up psychosis? So far from helping, it would be a disastrous end to his career. Perhaps he should suppress his report? Oh, to hell with it! He'd been over that possibility a hundred times before, and a hundred times he'd rejected it. His whole training was against it—suppressing a report was one of the things one just did not do.

Of course, his report would have one unusual feature to distinguish it. He hadn't merely spotted the U.F.O., he'd detected an electromagnetic transmission from it—in an unusual part of the wave band, too. Agent 38 couldn't understand why anyone should want to transmit at such a short wavelength. But after all, that wasn't his business. His business was to send out his report.

The transmission had obviously been coded. Although he himself hadn't been able to decipher it, perhaps the big bugs might be able to do so. Then perhaps they wouldn't think he was crazy. But the chances were they'd fail, just as he himself had failed. Which would put him in a tough spot. They'd think he'd invented the whole thing. They'd say that his psychosis was very very bad. He'd be moved immediately to some quiet place for recuperation.

Well, perhaps that wouldn't be so unpleasant after all. Perhaps deep down in himself that was what he really wanted. Perhaps that was the reason for his psychosis.

Dave Johnson looked out of the starboard porthole. There were four of them in the spaceship: Bill Harrison, Chris Yolantis, Stu Fieldman, and himself. This was the end of the line, the end of hard, unremitting training. But there were some things you could train for, and there were others you couldn't. Take the silence, for instance, the strange, gliding silence. It made you aware of all the little noises you could hear on Earth, even in places that were supposed to be dead quiet. For the first two weeks they'd played records and they'd talked incessantly. But then they'd come to realize they were talking simply to shut out the silence. After that it had seemed somehow better to accept the silence. So there were no long speeches anymore. Most of what they said now was in terse Anglo-Saxon.

Dave doubted that any of them had really recovered from the beginning. Once the shattering effect of the starting blast had worn off, they'd watched the bright ball of the Earth recede away from them. At first it had filled almost half the sky. But day after day it had become smaller and smaller. Now it was a mere point, like Mars or Jupiter. This was the terrible morale destroyer–watching your home receding implacably to huge, pitiless distances. You knew that out there, nearly forty million miles away, people were going about their daily lives–kids to school, commuters to work, housewives busying themselves, cars on the highways, hamburger stands. You knew it, but you couldn't believe it.

Soon another planet would be filling their sky. On paper everything was easy. They were to enter the atmosphere of Venus, brake down, descend below the white clouds, and then fly several times around. There wasn't to be a landing, because the scientists were quite certain Venus was covered entirely by ocean. Then they'd simply blast off again and return to Earth.

It was difficult to see where anything could go wrong. The reentry problem into the Earth's atmosphere had been solved years ago—they themselves had made four flights out from Earth during training. And entry into the Venusian atmosphere should be no different in principle from the case of Earth. The host of space vehicles encircling Venus over the past two decades had shown quite conclusively that the atmosphere contained nothing but harmless gases—nitrogen, carbon dioxide, and water.

Dave wondered just how far the ideas of the scientists would hold up. The clouds through which the spaceship must soon penetrate were thought to be merely frozen crystals of carbon dioxide—cirrus clouds of dry ice, in fact. But suppose the scientists were wrong. Suppose the clouds continued unbroken right down to the ocean surface. Suppose the oceans were boiling.

The blast-off from Venus would be controlled by radio transmitters on Earth. This was one comfort, at least. It would insure that the ship accelerated into the right orbit for the home trip. They themselves would be down under the Venusian clouds, unable to see out into space, certainly unable to choose the proper homeward trajectory. In fact, at any moment the people back home could take over control of the ship—a precaution just in case they all went crazy.

The spaceship began to bite into the atmosphere of Venus. The finlike wings began to be operated by the gas pressure outside.

Inside the ship, now that the long wait was over, the crew became rational and active. These were critical moments. Harrison, chief pilot, took over at the control panel.

"This is it boys," he growled. "This is what we came for."

They watched the speed indicator—down, down, always down. When the pointer reached half the initial entry reading, triumphantly they knew the rest was easy. It was only a matter of minutes now.

Then they were down to cruising speed, twelve hundred miles

per hour. Harrison adjusted the powerful motors–it needed little more than the idling rate to keep the speed steady, for the ship was held up now by aerodynamic lift from the gases through which it was moving, like an ordinary airplane.

The clouds below them appeared quite fantastically bright, far brighter than terrestrial clouds. The radio altimeter showed they were fifteen miles above the surface of the planet. Harrison set the ship in a gentle downward glide.

Thirteen miles up . . . eleven miles . . . into the clouds themselves. All eyes on the altimeter now. Dave knew just what the others were thinking: "Pray to Christ the thing is still okay." He noticed the temperature gauge–minus 75°C. outside–so low, the ship must still be high above the surface. The altimeter *was* okay.

Slowly the light intensity decreased. Nine miles up now. At seven miles they came suddenly out of the glaring white wall of cloud, to find that it was all fantastically similar to Earth–the blue glow below them caused by molecular scattering, the unbroken clouds far down there, probably water clouds lying over an ocean. There was one queer thing, though. The light was just about as bright as a clear sunlit day on Earth. But there was no sun here. For the sun was hidden now by the carbon dioxide clouds above them.

The crew whooped around the ship. They clapped one another on the back. There had been nothing to it at all, they roared. And there was nothing at all to what they still had to do. They'd only to fly a few times around this little fish tank. Then out into space again, back to Earth, back to fame–yes, back to FAME, in bright lights, boy. Man, ever since he *was* Man, had looked up at the sky, looked up at Venus–the Morning Star. But they, Dave Johnson and Company, were the first to *see* Venus–to come and claim the goddess for their own. Ecstatically, they gazed at the cloud below them. What did it cover?

Two hours later they found the first rifts. They caught a glimpse of a sea and they yelled in derisive appreciation of the scientists. The bastards had been right after all. But it was one thing to expound learnedly in a safe lecture room and it was quite something else to cross the gulf of space–forty million so-and-so miles of it, for Christ's sake.

At last, when they came toward the dark side of the planet, the lower clouds thinned and finally disappeared. In the evening light they could see a vast, apparently unlimited ocean below them.

It took a little more than five hours to cross the dark zone. Then, for two hours after reaching the dawnlit part of the planet, they found themselves again over open ocean. More low clouds with occasional rifts followed as they neared the subsolar regions.

After the first circuit, the flight became frankly boring. They would have liked to take the ship lower, but strict instructions were to stay above twenty-five thousand feet. Lower down, the atmospheric density was thought to be too high for a successful takeoff. And because they had no idea of exactly when the moment of takeoff would come, nobody felt tempted to risk dropping down to the ocean.

When the signal for takeoff did in fact come, after the third circuit, not one of them was sorry. It meant they'd gotten fifteen minutes to strap themselves in position, fifteen minutes before the body-searing acceleration hit them–fifteen minutes before they were on their way.

The seconds ticked off, lengthening imperceptibly into minutes. Dave Johnson wondered if he dare take a quick look at his watch. He decided against it. He decided that his judgment of time had gone haywire. With beating hearts they waited. They waited, listening to the purring motors. They waited tensely for a long time before one of them spoke. Yolantis said,

"I'm going to take a look, fellers."

They heard him move. If the motors fired now, Chris would be pulverized–literally pulverized. "Thirty-one minutes," they heard him mutter. Then Yolantis shouted out in terror. They found him at the main viewing-port. The ship was over clear ocean. They could see waves breaking, perhaps five thousand feet below. Harrison's face was deathly pale. "The controls are locked," he whispered. "The transmission from Earth must have gone all to hell. We're on a downward glide."

Should it be a quick death or a slow one? If they went in with the ship, they'd plummet instantly to the ocean bottom. If they launched the safety capsule, they'd probably be all right for a while. If the ocean was water, as it seemed to be, the capsule would float. They might be able to last out for a week or two. But it would come to exactly the same thing in the end. They had about five minutes to decide.

Perhaps they still had time to contact Earth? Pray to God that Earth could shift the controls at the very last minute.

Agent 38 watched the U.F.O. fall. He saw a small object, a capsule fastened to a parachute, break loose from it. Once he had found the correct transmission wave band and the right code, the U.F.O. had been almost absurdly easy to bring down. Exultantly, Agent 38 churned his huge whalelike body through the sea, the great transmitter in his head flashing electrical energy into the water.

There was very little salt in the water and his signals would travel a long way. Others would receive them and would come quickly to help him. Because of the eternal high cloud-cover, Agent 38 had never seen anything outside his planet. As he searched the waters methodically and rapidly, he found himself joyously wondering just what strange things he would find inside the capsule.

THE MARTIANS

The NASA budget in 1963 was something over 3.5 billion dollars. Twenty years later it was ten times more. Results justified the increase, not so much in spin-off to industry as in space itself. In the early days, a few prophets of disaster had openly stated their opinion, to the effect that no good of any kind would come out of the space program. By 1984 these dismal fellows had been given the lie. They were derided now as classic examples of fainthearted conservatism, the lack of broad vision which always seems to afflict the human species in some degree.

The first lunar mission achieved its objectives in 1973, only three years behind the original schedule. There were plenty of good reasons for this stretch-out. To begin with, the dust was really nasty stuff. It climbed all over you, head to toe, if you were unlucky enough to step into it. It climbed all over your equipment, into every crevice more than a few microns in size. The dust was like a liquid rising in a mass of capillary tubes, except that the forces were electrostatic, not surface tension. Unfortunately, the Moon has a lot of dust, so not too many places could be found where the first landing module might be safely set down. Indeed, the first pictures from the old Ranger project already showed only a few areas that appeared likely to be more or less free of dust. Later data from soft landings, some of them very soft, confirmed this. However, there were a few such areas, as it finally proved when the first men stepped gingerly out from their cabin. Everywhere around them was flat, hard ground, seemingly of dried-out mud.

The first landing didn't do much more than that. Down onto the deck, a judicious peek outside, then quickly back to the lunar-orbit rendezvous. Although it had cost the best part of one hundred billion bucks, hardly anybody now doubted that it had been well worthwhile. There was the usual bitching, it was true, from the high-energy physicists, who were having difficulty in acquiring a single lone billion, but once high-energy physics moved under the control of NASA that particular moan soon died away. Getting all funds for science under a single agency began to seem more and more like a good idea. It kept things in perspective and in proportion. It was tidy. The N.S.F. was also moved over.

Since glamour was now off the gingerbread, the second lunar mission had perforce to make up in effectiveness what it lacked in sensationalism. It went to the Moon to work, to survey, to dig, and to probe. The crew on this occasion included both a scientist-astronaut and a scientist-passenger. Ironically enough, the second landing turned out far more sensationally than the first. The disaster was noticed by the men in the rendezvous vehicle. Everything was quite normal for the first two days, they said, then suddenly the landing station was gone. In its place a new crater had appeared about three hundred yards in diameter. The precise mechanism of the disaster was unclear at the time, for it must have happened while the rendezvous vehicle was orbiting on the far side of the Moon. Later research showed, however, that the second landing party had been the unfortunate victims of what came to be known as a "soda squirt."

For a while there was discussion of cutting back the whole space program. But at length it was decided to press ahead with still greater vigor, in tribute to the space heroes, blown to perdition in some still-unexplained fashion.

Later missions very naturally proceeded with all due caution. It was discovered that ice lay below the dust and mud of the immediate surface of the Moon. There were huge glaciers shielded from space by the thin skin of dust. Wherever the skin was scraped away, the ice melted off into space very quickly. The temperature of the ice was found to increase with depth, which was natural, of course. This meant there must be liquid water low enough down. The water must be under pressure, a pressure generated by the weight of the overlying ice. Given any crack or hole in the solid glacier and, bingo, the water would stream explosively upward like an oil gusher. This was exactly what happened at places where the ice became exposed. More and more of the ice evaporated into space, until what remained became too thin to withstand the pressure of the liquid water below. So up came the water in a huge soda squirt. The water didn't settle back, it simply fizzed off into space.

These events were watched by the later expeditions from a safe distance. The precaution was necessary, for the rush of the water was extremely violent. Usually it shot out at a speed of about one mile per second, over three thousand miles per hour, sufficient to blow a small crater. It was now easily understood how the hitherto mysterious chains of small craters had been formed; they were strung along the courses of underground rivers, they were the places where the water had managed to punch through to the surface. In the gaunt, gray world of the Moon, the emergence of billions of tons of water was a fantastic and wonderful event, not at all like a terrestrial geyser. It was the colors you were aware of, a blaze of color that filled the whole sky.

The next step was to use the Moon for developing the techniques needed in the conquest of Mars. A permanent lunar laboratory was established. The essence of the business was to achieve self-sufficiency with the aid of regenerative life-support systems. For energy in its grosser forms, an interesting multistage method was used. For a start, a compact nuclear reactor was transported from Earth. This was used to power small diameter boreholes through the ice. So long as the water was allowed up only in small quantities, through a carefully constructed pipe, the flow could be kept under control. The critical thing was pressure at the surface. Instead of the water being permitted to spurt out freely into a vacuum, the pressure was taken down in several stages, in each of which the speed of the water was adjusted to match a set of turbines. Getting everything right in the beginning was very tricky indeed. However, once the difficulties were past, abundant energy was available in practically a permanent supply. Technically it was hydroelectric power, but on the Moon the water flowed uphill, not downhill, as on the Earth.

Oxygen came in ample quantities from the dissociation of water. Ultraviolet light from the Sun produced the dissociation, yielding nearly a kilogram of oxygen per day per square meter of exposed area. Ten square meters gave sufficient oxygen for a man. Nitrogen and carbon were problems, particularly nitrogen. The water from below had a lot of carbon dioxide dissolved in it, however. Really, it was soda. Less nitrogen, but enough, also came up with the water. Photosynthesis was quick and efficient, enabling a subsistence diet to become established. Trace elements, vitamins, and so on, were still imported from Earth. Even this dependence could have been overcome in time, but the time available for research on the Moon was now running out. As a NASA spokesman succinctly put it, the nation had acquired a Martian-wise capability.

It had come as a shock many years earlier to discover how very similar the Martian surface is to the Moon. This should really have been obvious from the beginning. It should have been obvious that the general dappled appearance of Mars is the same phenomenon as the "Man in the Moon" pattern of the lunar surface. The pattern comes from an overlapping of circular patches, like the "seas" or maria of the Moon, themselves produced by the large-scale impacts of huge meteorites, craters on the biggest scale of all. The canals that many observers thought they had seen turned out to be mere chains of craters. The human eye always tends to connect together a number of dots along a line, to see them as a complete line. This became obvious from the first fly-by pictures. Mars was simply a larger-scale version of the Moon.

This was why the lunar laboratory was so important. Much the same conditions could be expected on Mars, the same glaciers, the same water problems. Apart from the sheer dynamics of reaching Mars, demanding much more powerful boosters, apart from the length of the voyage—several months instead of days—most local problems should be less difficult on Mars. There would be somewhat stronger gravity, which was an advantage. The Martian atmosphere would remove the solar X-rays against which all lunar scientist-explorers had to be endlessly shrouded. There was some oxygen in the Martian atmosphere. Compressors would therefore give an adequate oxygen supply. The Martian atmosphere would reduce electrostatic effects so that dust would not be quite such a bad problem. The Martian atmosphere seemed to be an advantage in every way.

Both the atmosphere and the white polar caps of Mars were well understood now. With water coming up occasionally from below, exactly as on the Moon, thin polar caps of hoarfrost were just what one would expect. Martian gravity is intermediate between Earth and Moon. Terrestrial gravity is strong enough for the Earth to have retained most of the water squeezed from its interior throughout the eons. At the opposite extreme, the very weak lunar gravity of the Moon permits it to retain no surface water. Mars lies between. Mars holds water, but not for long. There is always a little water on the surface, water recently come from below which has not yet had time enough to escape away into space. The oxygen comes, of course, from dissociation of the water by sunlight, and carbon dioxide and nitrogen also come up with the water. The clouds observed from time to time by early astronomers were simply occasional squirts, released by an impacting meteorite from without. Mars was more subject to bombardment than the Moon, being nearer the asteroidal belt. Protecting spacecraft from impact was a serious difficulty, one that it didn't pay to think about too closely.

Mars was expected to be similar to the Moon in another respect, one which might well have served as a warning. A theoretical speculation dating from the 1960s was now entirely confirmed. Earth and Venus are both built from very roughly equal amounts of rock and unoxidized metals, particularly iron. The two components are largely separate, with the metals on the inside, the rocks on the outside, which raises the problem of how they got that way. Given a homogeneous, solid mixture of rock and metal in the first place, the metal would not sink to the middle. So much was realized. Perhaps when the planets were formed from a hot gas the metal was the first to condense. Then the rocks condensed later around the metal. This would solve the problem in one move. The trouble was that calculation showed rock and metal should both condense more or less together, as a mixture.

The solution came in a most surprising way. It was natural in the first calculations to assume the temperature of the cooling gases went steadily lower and lower as time went on. But this apparently reasonable hypothesis wasn't right. The temperature first went down, then it lifted for a while, before taking a final plunge in the last cooling phase. The temperature curve had first a minimum, then a maximum, after which it declined away. Condensation of rock and metal occurred equally at the minimum. The surprise came with a calculation which showed that although the rock and metal condensed together, they would not evaporate together at the succeeding temperature maximum. The metal would evaporate, but not the rock. So in the final decline of temperature it would be the metal that would condense bodily around the rock. Earth and Venus had the metal and rock separate, all right, but the wrong way round, the metal on the outside, not the inside.

This arrangement–an inner ball of rock surrounded by a substantially more dense shell of metal, the shell with a similar mass to the ball–was quite unstable, however. The shell collapsed inward, so that shell and ball interchanged themselves. The whole Earth was turned inside out, like Baron Munchausen's fox. The same was true for Venus, but not for the Moon or Mars. Neither the Moon nor Mars had very much metal, and what they had was still outside the rock. Their outer metallic shells had never become massive enough for the same instability to have occurred. A lot turned on the difference, on Mars having its metal on the outside.

With space technology developed to a state of planet-wise capability, and with the mass of data collected from the many telepuppets now in orbit around the planet, the stage was set for a manned mission to Mars. Although the astronauts assigned to the mission were as dedicated as ever, they were naturally much worried by the sterility problem.

The first lunar rockets had possessed no more than a certified sterility. Used for soft landings, they were dealt with by simple ethylene-oxide techniques. The priority was soon off the sterility problem, however, so far as the Moon was concerned. Cynthia turned out to be herself entirely sterile. No wonder, with the drenching of X-rays she was receiving, and with the cold on her backside and the heat on her frontside. Thereafter nobody had any worries about "ejecta" on the Moon.

Mars was another breed of cats. Twenty years earlier, Mars

had already been declared a biological preserve. This had been agreed internationally. As one cognizant biologist put it, "The mere suggestion that fecal material might be jettisoned under conditions which would contaminate the surface is symptomatic of attitudes which fail to give appropriate consideration of exobiological objectives." Such irresponsible procedures were condemned, totally and emphatically. In plain language, readily understandable to one and all, this meant you couldn't shit on Mars.

A tremendous amount of research, it is true, had been put into the development of space suits equipped with really efficient "biological barriers," as the pundits of NASA put it. Be this as it may, all astronauts found these things the very devil. It seemed much simpler to go chronically constipated.

Then come the problem of back-contamination, not that there seemed much chance of pathogens existing on Mars. Nobody at NASA was ever known to call a spade a spade, or to use a simple word where a complicated one would do. In plain language, again, precautions had to be taken against a "bug" being imported back from Mars. So it came about that an incredibly complex quarantine "machinery" was set up. It wasn't just a matter of keeping the returning astronauts in isolation for some defined period. After all, any bugs that happened to be inside them had already been cooking for three months or more, throughout the return voyage. It was more that the astronauts had to be "degaussed," that is, to have the contents of the intestinal tract entirely removed, the blood supply withdrawn and replaced, and so forth, all by glove-box techniques.

The first Martian mission was given over to glamour, just like the first lunar mission. It was a case of nipping down from orbit, nipping for a little while out onto the planet itself, nipping back into the module—a quite fat job, this time—and of nipping up again into orbit. Three months out from Earth, three months back, unconscionable thick lumps of bread enclosing an excessively thin slice of meat. Still, the first expedition already cast doubt on the "life on Mars" theory. Not a bug, not a protein, not an amino acid, or any conceivable biochemical relation thereof, was found in the samples brought back to Earth.

The cognizant biologists took a bad knock. They had pushed a lot of people around, spent a lot of money, and achieved precisely nothing. Goaded into a last spasm, they insisted that further tests be made. Although very extensive samplings were taken by the second mission, not a trace of organic material was found. Life did not exist on Mars. Thereafter the planet was given over to the scientist-explorers.

Nothing really epoch-making was expected. Yet the instinct to stand where nobody has stood before is strong in all of us. The third mission set about its task of establishing a long-term Martian station with zest and zeal. Preliminary to setting up a permanent energy supply, the same boring down through the underground glaciers was put in hand. It had all been done before, but not there on Mars. This made the mission interesting and worthwhile.

A great discovery was made during a lull in these preliminary operations. Instruments deep below the surface found sound waves propagating everywhere throughout the ice of the glaciers. Records were immediately flashed back to Earth. They were processed in the NASA laboratories. The amplitude and frequency patterns were definitely not random. Highly complex variations were repeated from time to time, making it virtually certain that the sound waves must be information-carrying. But what, and to whom, and from where? Instructions to the third mission were to keep on transmitting the sound patterns back to Earth and to "proceed" with all due caution.

Here were Martians at last. It was a good story, told with febrile intensity by press, radio, and T.V. The NASA top brass allowed themselves to be dug up for the occasion. This was the very lifeblood of their budget. It was gravely emphasized that timely and responsible decisions would be made, just as soon as the analysis now in progress had ingested the situation.

Actually, nobody was getting anywhere toward cracking the code of the sound signals, which just went on and on without cease, night and day, week after week. If only somebody could have had an idea, an idea for making one single rational contact with the stuff. Then a second contact might have been possible, followed by a third, and so on. But nothing whatsoever came of all the writhing and thrashing.

When the news media saw how the mountain labored, they dropped the whole thing like a hot potato. Time enough to wrestle with the Martian problem as soon as there was something or someone to wrestle with. So the massive-hearted, palpitating public got itself back to the latest aspects of sex-worship.

By 1984 the stories currently popular on the screen would have seemed pretty ripe material to an earlier generation. Entertainment had been enjoying an apparently never-ending boom, a boom soundly based on affluence and leisure. Yet as it grew, the entertainment industry destroyed itself by consuming, like a fantastic lotus-eating dinosaur, the very material on which it depended for its existence. By now it seemed as if every idea had been flogged to death, as indeed it had. Suspense stories were the hardest hit of all. With each succeeding year, sensation had to be piled on sensation. By 1970, the successes of 1965 seemed woefully out of date. By 1975, it was exactly the same way with the successes of 1970. The human race was steadily becoming "sophisticated," it was burning out its natural responses, first to more or less normal situations, then to abnormal ones, then to utterly pathological ones.

Every so often someone came up with a really new gimmick. Then you always kicked yourself for not having seen it first yourself. Gimmicks no longer needed to be clever. The important thing was to be quite new. Like snow in May, they didn't last long, but while they lasted, you did all right.

It was easy to understand why in these circumstances sex had become such an intensely marketable commodity. This was the major field of entertainment now, because it was the one field in which originality was not important. Evolution proceeded, not by increased sophistication, but by increased display, by an increased emphasis on realism, the very opposite from the suspense area. Unrelenting pressures from a wealthy industry had forced censorship into retreat after retreat, until by now all attempts at control had virtually broken down. Against sex, the Martian story barely made it as a nine-days' wonder.

Yet there was something on Mars, something below the glaciers. It was reasonable to suppose that, whatever it was down below, there were several of them, for they seemed to be communicating one to another with the aid of the sound in the ice. They used sound in ice perhaps like we use sound in air. It made sense, so far. But continued failure to establish any kind of link with the Martians eventually set up a frustration complex, both in the scientist-explorers themselves and at NASA headquarters. Injection of man-made sound into the ice was tried at an early stage. It produced no apparent response, although it was never made clear quite what response could have been expected.

Many theories about the Martians were advanced. They were all outrageous, but of course even the correct theory had to be outrageous. Any explanation for an intricate system evolving out of an initially simple situation must always seem outrageous. Nothing could be more so than the story of biological evolution here on the Earth—to an outsider, to a Martian, say. It is usual for complex situations to collapse into simpler ones, not the other way round. Most theories were due to cranks who completely missed this point: How does one invert the usual time sense of natural events? How does one get simplicity evolving into complexity?

The importance of metals near the surface of Mars, metals below the glaciers, was first noticed by a theoretician. Not all the metal would be the same stuff. Because of the different work functions of different metals, there would be contact potentials. Next, what were the important volatiles liberated from the interior of a planet? In order of decreasing quantity: water, carbon dioxide, chlorine, nitrogen. Water and chlorine could give you hydrochloric acid. Different metals in acid gave you an electric current.

How much energy could be expected? Reckoning a depth of electrolyte, say of one hundred meters, at least an equal depth for the metallic skin, taking 10^9 erg for the output per gram of material, the grand energy total came out at 10^{31} erg, equivalent to the output of about ten trillion tons of coal and oil, not much different from the actual coal and oil reserves of the Earth. This could be a minimum estimate. The actual energy total could be one to two orders of magnitude higher still.

These ideas were first put forward at a meeting of the National Academy of Sciences in Washington. The biologists wanted to know their relevance. Maybe there *was* an electrical storage battery on Mars, so what? Energy wasn't the same thing as life, although admittedly it was necessary to life. A coal mine, or an oil well, wasn't alive just because there was energy in it. The point seemed well taken, but the reply was also well taken—in some quarters, at least.

A coal mine wasn't alive because for one thing the energy was in a bad form. Coal had to be burned to release the energy, and the heat was disorganized. Electricity was much better, it could be converted directly into controlled motion. Everybody knew this perfectly well. You plugged devices in the home, like a shaver, into the electric supply, not into the boiler—at least you did if you were a physicist. No cognizant biologist liked this crack. Okay, you have an "electric motor" on Mars, so what?

Well, with controlled motion the logical possibility existed for a feedback between the motion and the flow of electricity. In principle, it was possible for the system to affect itself. In view of the tremendous amount of energy that must be released on Mars, it was quite *un*reasonable to suppose feedback never happened. Evolution by selection was then just as possible in an electrical system as in a chemical one. It was no more unlikely for complicated surface effects to arise, complicated circuits under continuous modification, than it was for complicated molecules leading to living cells to develop. The principle of competition for the available energy supply, whether chemical or electrical, was the same. The basic logic was the same, and it was this that really counted, not the realization of the logic in practical terms. To push the argument further, it was biological evolution that was really inefficient and rather stupid. First a complex chemical system—the cell—had to be produced. Then cells were put together into what were still chemical assemblies. Only at a late stage did the interesting things happen, with the development of the brain. Wasn't it through the brain that we think, make judgments, feel emotion? What is the brain but an electrical instrument? Terrestrial biology had evolved through a lot of cumbersome chemistry before it reached the real point, the electronics. On Mars, it had been electronics all the way.

The popular news media were back on the job now. Displaying to the full their twin characteristics, incredible persistence and incredible inability to see the point, they clamored for an answer to the absurd question: Could Martian computers be said to be really alive? The theoretician, hopelessly harassed by every newspaper from the *Herald* to the *Calgary Eye-Opener,* by gangs of men—camera men, sound men, photographers—who had descended on his home, replied that since life was no more than organized data-processing, in accordance with some preassigned program, this could be done just as well by a computer as by a human. He was asked to put it in terms that could be understood by the ordinary housewife. Well, hadn't a computer just won the world's chess championship? But was winning a chess game the same thing as being alive? Anyway, wasn't it necessary to instruct a computer about how to play chess? Wearily, the theoretician explained that humans too were instructed, they had been programed by millions of years of evolution. In any case, what was the aim of a commercial on T.V., what was the aim of an ad in the newspapers? Surely to program people.

The battery and computer theory wasn't widely believed at first, because the sound waves in the ice appeared to contradict it. Why would sound waves be used in an electrical system? Not for communication. No system of computers would communicate with each other by sound, not unless the situation on Mars was even more crazy than it seemed to be. One feature of the theory was attractive to NASA, though. It supported a step to which the scientist-administrators were already strongly inclined, to continue the borehole which had been instantly stopped when the signals were first discovered. The thing to do next, it now seemed, was to discover what kind of liquid lay below the ice, if indeed there was any liquid.

When the hole was completed, instead of a soda squirt, there came a powerful great squirt of filthy, evil-smelling stuff containing chlorine, bromine, and H_2S. This was a bad blow to the prospects of a permanent Martian laboratory, but at least it supported the electrolyte theory. Yet the sound signals were still a puzzle.

The puzzle was solved at last in a singular fashion. One morning the scientist-explorers were astonished to find a shining, cigar-shaped machine standing outside the laboratory. In one side of it they could see an opening, as if a panel had been slid back. Gingerly, in a frankly suspicious frame of mind, they examined the object as best they could without actually entering it. Nothing of any kind, no projection of any sort, was to be discovered on the exterior. It was all completely smooth, a metallic alloy of some kind. A periscopic device was used to examine the interior–so that nobody need enter the thing. Absolutely nothing could be seen. There was no control console inside. It was all completely smooth.

At least the machine looked quite harmless, unless there were more panels behind which weapons of some kind were lurking. Full information was sent immediately to Earth. Instructions came back, to the effect that the scientist-explorers should proceed with extreme caution, but that reasonable enterprise should not be eschewed.

The machine lay completely static outside the laboratory for several days. The men looked it over for the hundredth time. Obviously the damn thing had arrived with some kind of intent but had then got itself stuck. It just stood there day after day, with an opening in one side. Two men got into it together, so that if anything happened there would be two of them to deal with it. Nothing happened. There seemed nothing that could happen, since there were no controls—and even if there had been controls, there was nobody to operate them. The two got out, quite safely. The others went in and out, one after the other. It was all apparently quite safe. Yet on the very last man the door closed, without making the slightest sound, not a click or a rustle. The thing moved smoothly away. There was nothing at all that could be done to stop it. The lucky ones watched as it moved forward, at no great pace, for three or four hundred yards. Then it turned at an angle, so that it looked rather like a torpedo launched from an airplane. Like a torpedo it disappeared from sight, into the ice that lay below.

The following morning the machine was back again, the door in its side open once more. Nobody ventured into it this time. They took welding torches to it. As soon as the heat began to play on the metal, the machine moved away for a few yards, rather as a cow might step away from a bunch of flies on its rump. The men followed it for a while, trying to get their instruments to work on it. Always it moved just a little way ahead of them, as if it was playing some kind of game, or trying to lead them someplace. At last they got fed up and left it alone. Within an hour it was back on their doorstep.

All these events were transmitted to Earth, along with the record of the sound waves. Immediately following the incident in which the machine made off, Europa-like, with the unfortunate scientist-explorer, the amplitude of the sound was found to be very high. From this it was deduced that the sound waves were simply a form of sonar, used by the machine as it bored its way down through the glacier. Two other points were clear. The machine was only a slave-robot sent by the real Martians to collect samples of whatever it was that had arrived on their planet. From the complexity of the sound waves, it was also evident there must be very many such machines. Probably the interior of the glacier was honeycombed by passages along which they moved in the fashion of subway trains. The sonar was obviously used for navigational purposes and to prevent collisions of one machine with another, and perhaps to prevent them from penetrating into the intricate electronic system of the Martians themselves. Presumably the latter were quite static, like terrestrial computers, the robots being used for mechanical communication.

A warning was sent from Earth, to the effect that the scientist-explorers should expect to have to deal with more than one of these slave-machines. Caution should be exercised. The warning was superfluous. Something approaching a hundred cigar-shaped machines had already surrounded the laboratory. The urgent question now was whether the mission could extricate itself at all. On every side a mass of shining metal could be seen. Gradually, almost cautiously, the machines began to close in, a foot or two at a time, in a kind of slow, shuffling movement.

There was nothing to be done except run for it. The men waited until the gleaming monsters were quite close. At first it didn't seem too bad, because in the weak gravity of Mars they could jump clean over the brutes. The machines responded as if it were only some kind of game. Instead of each machine searching separately for the men, the things worked in a team, apparently in accord with some master plan. They sought to block each of the men, working on data from the sound waves generated in the ground by the men in their flight, or so it seemed. Certainly the machines were not equipped with apparatus sensitive to light. They could not see. When the men stopped, the machines stopped. But as soon as a man took a single step, the machines glided into some new pattern.

Four of the men made it, three did not. From the safety of the module, the four lucky ones watched in horror as each of the three was cornered, hemmed in by packed lines of machines which could not be jumped. The things built a quadrangle about each man, in turn. One machine went into the quadrangle along with the man. The last desperate struggle took a long time, but always it ended the same way, with the man pushed over, sprawling on the ground. The machine rolled over on top of him, but with a door open. The unfortunate victim found himself precipitated into the quite smooth capsule inside the monster. Inevitably, the door closed. The machine with the prize in its belly then began its journey to the depths below. The other machines opened out to make a way for it. The thing moved to a middle distance. Suddenly it tilted and disappeared.

All this came out after the return of the residue of the third Martian mission. NASA didn't like it. Nobody liked it. Everybody felt the expedition should have been armed with nuclear weapons. Yet NASA could hardly be blamed for its failure to anticipate the existence of developed Martians. Cognizant biologists had expected only to collect a few bugs or, at best, a few primitive plants.

Preparations were put in hand to plug a batch of nuclear weapons into the surface of Mars. After considerable argument, however, it was decided to wait awhile. For one thing, it wasn't clear how the Martians, deep below their glaciers, could be harmed by surface explosions. For another, the Martians hadn't really done anything explicitly hostile. Certainly four perfectly sound citizens had been creamed. Yet look at it from the other side for a moment. Four perfectly sound Martians had probably been sucked up through the borehole drilled by the third mission. Squirting Martians into the atmosphere in the style of a soda siphon would naturally be viewed in a grave light by the other side. Surely it would justify an examination of the situation, even to the extent of hunting down one or two of the strange creatures that had suddenly appeared out of space. We ourselves would hardly have acted in any other way. Whichever way you looked at it, nuclear weapons wouldn't have much effect, not a kilometer or two down.

The telepuppets came into their own at this stage. They were set to watch the Martian surface by electronic camera. A stream of pictures was telemetered to Earth. It soon appeared that remarkable changes were in hand. Large structures appeared, very like radio antennae. It made sense when you came to think about it. Perhaps for millions of years the Martians had lived under their glaciers without experiencing any visitation from outside. Possibly from time to time they had taken a look at the external world, finding little of interest. It was very different now, however. At last there had indeed been a visitation from outside, and the Martians were determined to find out, what the hell. NASA had succeeded, at fantastic expense, in stirring a hornet's nest.

Yet there was nothing to worry about when the first signals came through. Attempts were made to decode them, of course, but without the slightest success. Somebody had the amusing idea of setting up a closed loop. There seemed no possibility of it doing any harm. Signals from Mars were fed directly into a terrestrial computer, the output from which was fed back to a terrestrial transmitting antenna, back to Mars. Nobody expected much to come of it, but everybody hoped for something more than a simple return of the original message. Small changes, in fact, appeared after a few days. The terrestrial computer was not returning exactly the same signals as the ones which were being fed into it. This meant the home computer was acting as an outpost for the Martians, although of course in an apparently harmless way. The Martians must have discovered something of the home computer's function and of its basic design.

The next step was to investigate what was going on. It was necessary now to work the closed loop through the home computer with a man-made program inside it. So the loop was set up in parallel with a straightforward mathematical problem. It was a simple matter of time-sharing, the computer being used for two apparently quite distinct purposes, much as one can run two distinct human problems in the same computer at the same time. Whereas the human problems stay distinct, however, these did not. The Martian loop stopped the mathematical problem. There wasn't any mystery about how this could happen. The Martians stopped the mathematics in exactly the same way we ourselves would do, by instructions to the computer from without. There was no difficulty about it and apparently no harm either. Indeed, it was all very encouraging, since it implied a small area of contact with the Martians. Further experiments were tried out with varying success. Other kinds of human program were used. Chess, in which the Martians took not the slightest interest, business accountancy and general data-processing, language translation, and so forth, traffic-flow problems. A lot of stuff was put on tape and the Martians were left to sort it out as best they could.

Two things occurred in quick succession. The computer started to work in earnest, in a very different fashion from its earlier sporadic behavior. Instructions were inserted for a print-out of the contents of the computer, but the print-out proved to be on a hopelessly vast scale. There was no possibility of detecting any sense in it. The other thing was that pictures from the telepuppets ceased. A meteorite might have hit one of them, but the whole lot could hardly have been hit all at exactly the same time. The Martians had evidently knocked them off, there could be no other explanation.

Preparations for meeting an invasion from Mars were now put seriously in hand. The nuclear defense capability was weighed and not found wanting. There seemed no grounds for alarm. Nobody thought to break the computer link with Mars. The link was indeed thought of as an advantage, since it could eventually give a lead to the purposes and the nature of the Martians.

The invasion came without any notice at all. The stuff was sprinkled into the terrestrial atmosphere as if from a cosmic pepper pot. The Martians treated chemistry rather as humans treat electronics, something to be worked out by rational calculation, not a subject for crude empiricism. With their vast calculating resources, the properties of complex molecules could be definitively worked out. So they knew exactly what they were doing when the stuff was sprinkled into the terrestrial atmosphere. It took the best part of three months for it to settle to ground level and to get into water supplies all over the Earth. Then there was the devil to pay. The birth rate fell to zero within a few more weeks. The human species suddenly found itself completely sterile, in fantastic contrast to its previous cornucopian fecundity. The chemical makeup of the bodies of the unfortunate scientist-explorers had given all the necessary data. The determination of a complete inhibitor of human fertility had then been a straightforward, if somewhat tedious, job.

The species was left to savor the situation for a couple of months. Everybody was by then convinced that complete biological extinction was the Martian aim. Everybody settled into this belief with a dull, resigned hopelessness. Then came the first full and lucid print-out from the computer, the one in contact with the Martians. Instructions were given for the construction of several hundred robot machines. There was nothing apparently harmful in the specifications; it was obvious these robots could be physically overwhelmed at a moment's notice if need be. Preparations for their construction were put in hand. There was nothing else to be done. The first ones off the line turned out rather jolly little fellows, with big, square boxes on top of the short, stumpy legs. They were just mobile computers, not at all complicated, even by terrestrial standards. Yet they had one special ability, they were far more efficient intermediaries between humans and the bigger computer, the one in constant contact with the Martians, than our own input-output devices could ever have been.

No sooner did the robots begin work than babies began to be born again. The total birth rate was still extremely low, far too low for any kind of stability in the human population, but it was something to find even a ray of hope in what had appeared an impossibly black situation. The game was still not played out.

Further robots were built to new specifications. They were bigger now and there were more of them. This second generation was industrially inclined. It collected scads of data. It gave rational, clear instructions on what was to be done. More and more of the new machines moved into executive offices. In evidence of the good faith of the Martians, the birth rate continued to rise little by little. Young women everywhere were much in favor of the new situation. Not only was there a better chance now of a small family, but their husbands had been ejected from the offices in which previous decades of husbands had entombed themselves. Babies had to be worked for harder, of course, but was there anything very much wrong in that?

The third robot generation was quite different again. To the jolly little communication chaps, and the efficient industrial chaps, there was now added a policeman-robot. These fellows were literally tougher than nails, much much tougher than gangsters and F.B.I. men had been, much tougher even than the agents of pure fiction. You could certainly blow them apart with high explosive, but you couldn't knock them off with a pistol. They were much much stronger than a gorilla. With a single blow they could explode you like a bag of water.

The policemen-robots had no sense of justice, or of mercy, or of pity. Neither had they any spirit of vindictiveness, any lust for revenge or vengeance. They were not sadistic, nor did they give themselves airs. Nor did they rape your sister. They knew and cared about just one thing, instruction and obedience. So long as you obeyed an instruction you were okay. If you disobeyed, you were given one single opportunity for reconsideration. If you then obeyed, okay, if not, wham—a heavy metal ball flew at enormous speed along an arc in the style of a medieval joust.

Nobody liked the policemen-robots, yet in some ways they turned out better than the jolly little communication chaps. As soon as plots began to hatch against the new order, the communication chaps, with their stumpy legs and big heads, showed themselves to have a real genius for sniffing out what you were up to. They were never unpleasant about it, of course, for it was apparently not their place to usurp the functions of the policemen-robots.

The policemen-robots were always pretty fair. Once they had broken a thing up, once the conspirators were scattered, the ruckus was instantly forgotten. Ringleaders were never sorted out as examples. Your past record was never held against you. There were no blacklists. To a policeman-robot there was just one single issue, whether you obeyed the current instruction or you did not. So far as anyone could tell, the policemen-robots never troubled to remember you, they simply served to distinguish obedience from disobedience. This made them surprisingly easy to take. You had no feeling of losing face when you obeyed, no feeling of the robot getting any satisfaction from your obedience. To a robot it was just as unemotional as deciding whether or not one hundred is greater than ninety-nine. If it was, okay. If it wasn't, wham. There was indeed a curiously restful quality about the policemen-robots. In place of the appalling psychological complexities of humans, you knew exactly where you were with these big ten-foot chaps standing over you. It took you back to childhood, as if Daddy was still looking down on you.

It was in any case rather like religion. You did what the priest told you to do under pain of hell-fire. Here you did it under pain of the big black jousting ball. Like a priest, these robots had an intense devotion to right and wrong. There was no doubt about their having a vocation.

As the robots gained power, serious dissension broke out

between the sexes. To women, sterility was bad enough, even on an individual basis. On a worldwide scale, it was an appalling and obscene horror, not to be contemplated if any alternative were possible. Women everywhere were wholeheartedly in favor of accepting the rule of the Martians. Nobody was being hurt by it. In any case, the men had brought it all on themselves by their incessant yap-yapping about power and progress, by their sheer smugness, in fact.

The men were not even able to diagnose their complaint, let alone cure it. The advance of technology had already made it more and more difficult to give satisfactory expression to the inherent apelike demands of the dominant male. The male ape attempts the suppression of every ape of its own kind within sight or smell. It attempts the suppression of every male ape by physical violence and intimidation, of every female ape by physical violence and sex. From the nineteenth century onward, it was known that man is an ape. Everybody knew this was so, but nobody believed it was so. It was true but it wasn't really true. In a sufficiently primitive technological state, humans will separate themselves into groups, the size of the group being exactly determined by the criterion that the dominant male of the moment shall be able to assert his dominance in person directly over every other member of the clan. Forced by technology into larger units, the dominant male, now the king, will perforce be obliged to delegate a considerable fraction of his over-apeness to certain immediate under-apes, known as barons. This aristocracy will pass on the king's dominance at second-hand to still lower under-apes. Second-hand is second-best, the over-ape loses satisfaction from this delegation of his dominance. To make good his losses, he engages now in violent demonstrations of his superiority, by orgies, by torture, by gladiatorial combats, by executions, and by war.

Under-apes are surprisingly happy. They can easily understand the psychology of the over-ape. Even in the interval between blows they have time to realize that they themselves would gladly wield the whip if things were the other way round. Down in the breast of even the humblest there is always the irrational hope that he too may one day become an over-ape.

With the development of industrial techniques, the basic cravings of the male were forced deeper underground. They were forced into pallid politics, and into a chase after power that was not really power. With the rise of the Martian robots, the cravings of the male were at last wholly suppressed. The robots were taking comparatively little away from the women. From the men they were taking everything of real importance. True, the men had lost nothing economically, quite the reverse, but they had lost the last shams of political power, the last shreds of boardroom–and even bedroom–dominance.

To the men, the destruction of the robots was fast becoming urgent. Early on, the men had given way in order to placate the women. Now, before it was too late, they insisted in revolting utterly and completely against Martian dominance. The robots capitulated without even a struggle, probably because a careful calculation showed they couldn't win at that time. There was no Horatio-at-the-Bridge attitude about them, no "face" to save, no problem of "morale" to worry about. If the battle couldn't be won, there was no point in fighting it.

Only a small percentage of the men understood the critical point, that the robots weren't the real Martians. It had been said often enough, of course, that the real Martians were still on Mars, underneath their protective glaciers. But this was too remote and abstract for the average man. Nobody had dug up the glaciers and looked underneath, had they? So how could you be sure? It was hard not to credit a machine with intelligence, not when it showed intelligence. It may be understood, then, how it was that most men took great pleasure in the destruction of the robots. They cooked the jolly communication chaps by throwing them into a furnace, where they soon melted into "juice." The business-robots, after dismemberment, were left outdoors to oxidize, slowly. For the policemen-robots they reserved special compactors, built after the pattern of machines used for compacting automobiles. The robots were fed in as robots at one end. They emerged at the other end as neat cubes, jousting ball and all. Before they were impelled into the compactor, the robots were shown the emerging cubes. It was always a disappointment that, while every robot continued to display an intelligent interest in what was going on, this demonstration never put a single robot in the least out of countenance. No robot was ever known to emit the smallest Petrushka-like cheep.

The bottom fell out of the birth rate, right down to zero. All along, this was what the women had said would happen. The birth rate didn't get off the floor until the men started to build robots again. Wearisomely, the pattern was repeated, first the communication chaps, then the business tycoons, then the policemen-robots to keep everything neat and tidy. Inevitably, there was a second revolt. Inevitably, the birth rate zeroed. Inevitably, the pattern was repeated, and repeated again.

This was all part of the plan. The Martians wanted the human population down, not down to nothing at all, but to manageable proportions. This meant a reduction by a very big factor. Without establishing fantastic slaughterhouses, it was clearly necessary to wait forty or fifty years for the existing population to die off in peace and prosperity. Replacements were kept at a low level, only about one hundred thousand a year for the whole species. Even this meager yield had to be worked hard for. It became an all-out effort for the men. The Martians were clever enough not to arrange one hundred thousand pregnancies per annum, regardless. More subtly, they worked on the basis of one pregnancy per N copulations, with N adjustable to give the required annual crop of one hundred thousand babies. In the early days, N was kept fixed, so that everybody then got it firmly into their heads that the more sex, the more babies. With this belief established, the Martians increased N more and more, as manufacturers used to do in their old time-and-motion studies. Like the old manufacturers, the Martians never reduced N. Once they discovered the sex-wise capability of the human species, they kept them to it.

The men were actually reduced to making a complaint, through the agency of the jolly communication chaps, when at one time things really had gone a bit far. The Martians replied in the following terms:

(1) A survey of the entertainment enjoyed by the human species throughout the second half of the twentieth century shows that sex served as the major item of human attention, pleasure, and happiness.

(2) The pursuit of happiness is the declared intent of the human species.

(3) Present policy provides for (2).

(4) The subject is closed.

The sheer physical strain of maintaining what turned out to be a stable population of some three million reduced the men to a state in which they no longer had the necessary determination to suppress the robots. A critical point was passed, separating the time when the robots might once again have been consigned to the furnace and to the compactor from the final era in which this was no longer possible. The jousting ball was now ultimate law. The human species was powerless, not only biologically, but also physically. The Martians had won the final battle, and without striking a single physical blow, if one excepts the biochemical analysis of the four unfortunate scientist-explorers sent to them at such enormous expense by NASA. Humans had themselves looked after the physical aspects of the matter, even to the extent of building the robots which now held them in bondage. It only remained for the Martians to have the robots herd the whole human species together into a reasonably spacious compound. Earth could then be cleaned up, cleaned of its horrible green slime, and at last made fit for a Martian to live in.

So it came about that the entire human species came to live in greater Los Angeles, and that true Martians arrived here to take up an abode beneath the polar icecaps. Ample water was pumped in to the humans, who kept their little patch of

Earth forever verdant. There were just a few who hankered after the strident old days, but they never got much of a hearing. Life on the whole was very pleasant. Indeed, there came a time when the species attained a considerable cachet. Rather to their own surprise, the Martians found humans a distinctly exportable item. Nobody throughout the Galaxy could at first believe it possible for such astonishing creatures to exist. Nobody had ever conceived of chemical life. As far as was known, the creatures were quite unique.

SHORTSIGHTED

The spring of 1966 brought startling news to the British bird-watching world. A pair of Baird's Oreales were nesting in the park of an estate near Bury Saint Edmunds.

Hugh McAlan was an improbable bird-watcher. Seriously shortsighted, he was a convert to the eye-exercise school. Bird-watching had been recommended to him as likely to sharpen his acuity. It did so, but not for the reason McAlan imagined. There was no improvement at all in the optics of the eye. What bird-watching did was to make him more consciously aware of the information that was passing in any case from eye to brain, information which he had previously ignored. It simply directed certain things to his attention, things that had been there anyway.

SHORTSIGHTED

McAlan applied to the Ornithological Trust for a permit to visit the estate near Bury Saint Edmunds. He wasn't too hopeful about his application, because it was plainly impossible for the Trust to grant permits to more than a small fraction of the many ornithologists of the Greater London area. Hugh McAlan was one of the lucky ones as it turned out, however. He was given a permit for eleven A.M. Sunday, which was much the best day of the week for him, and pretty well the best time of day, too.

So one morning in late April, McAlan headed his Austin Mini out of London onto the Newmarket-Bury road. By his side were binoculars and a luncheon satchel, in the boot of the car his faithful waders.

The ornithological party, when fully assembled, turned out to be about fifty strong. With so many people, the warden who conducted them through the estate was understandably reluctant to approach the Oreales closely. At all costs, the birds must not be frightened from the park.

Some of the party claimed to have sighted the Oreales in the far distance, but McAlan wasn't one of them. He saw a white-backed woodpecker, a nuthatch, and a redstart, which partly made up for the Oreales. The session lasted several hours. His feet were quite tired by the time he got back to the Mini.

Hugh McAlan decided to return along the Haverhill road instead of by the faster A 11. He started off down quiet country lanes, musing to himself. He wasn't giving full attention to the driving, but neither was he really careless. He would have noticed any unexpected road traffic, like a car pulling out of a side road, for instance. What he did not notice, until it was too late, was a pair of birds, flying endlessly round and around each other, a pair that came into the road over the bushes on his near side. There was an unpleasant thud as the car hit the wretched creatures. Only after the impact was McAlan fully aware of what had happened. He stopped and looked back over his shoulder. The birds were lying dead in the road, the road itself covered by an incredibly vast carpet of feathers. He climbed slowly out of the car and sadly walked to the point of the tragedy. Some of the feathers were of a greenish tinge. There were black tailfeathers, too. But most were of a brilliant yellow. Hugh McAlan had "got" his Oreales after all.

A JURY OF FIVE

Arthur Hadley was a hard-driving man, just turned fifty. His only occupations were business and sex. On these topics he lavished his working hours in a ratio of about three to one. His headquarters were in Nottingham, but his activities were by no means confined to the immediate neighborhood. He had a chain of interests spread over the whole of the north of England. He had partners in some of these interests, partners whom he terrified by the risks he ran, like Tony Brown. Sir Anthony Brown was a yellow-bellied twerp, in Hadley's personal opinion, but his title happened to be useful. The risks were always of the "swallow-all-the-water-in-the-sea" kind. Hadley's specialty was the take-over bid. Early in life he'd discovered a simple truth, take-overs go most smoothly and profitably if they're done when times are bad. There was no point in making bids for prosperous firms with long order books, too costly. In the old days, he'd bought when trade was slack. Now things were different, without the old big ups and downs. He bought now when credit was tight, and credit was tight every three or four years, whenever the whole country got itself into another kettle of economic hot water. In the year 1965 he did quite a lot of buying. By the end of 1965 he was pretty replete, overextended, folks called it. For the next year or two it would be necessary to sit down and work away at it all, to chew the cud, to masticate.

Arthur Hadley was good at chewing the cud, because he gave a lot of time and thought to the process. He was good at choosing the right man for a job. He made mistakes sometimes, of course, but once he realized he'd made one, he always put it right quickly. "Cut your losses—fast" was one of his favorite tags. He was thinking now of hoofing out a dull old bugger, who for donkey's years had run a firm he'd recently bought on the outskirts of Sheffield. Too set in his ways, too stereotyped, too old-fashioned. The only problem was, who to move into the job. Perhaps it would be best to give young Mike Johnson a whirl. It would mean taking him away from the Nottingham factory, which would be a real nuisance just at the moment. But he couldn't see a better solution. He said so to his twenty-eight-year-old wife, Jennifer, and was surprised when Jenny disagreed. Usually she just listened to his business talk. He used her as a pair of ears, not really because he needed to talk to anybody, for advice or anything like that, but because he was inhibited—like most people—against talking to himself. That was why he was surprised about Mike Johnson. For a brief flash he wondered whether there could be anything between Johnson and his wife. Then he dismissed the thought. Jenny hadn't much appetite for that sort of game.

Like many promiscuous men, Hadley expected his wife to be one hundred percent "respectable." Wasn't that one of the reasons why he'd married her, for Christ's sake? The daughter of a local manufacturer, Jennifer had been well-educated. She was well-spoken and she knew how to entertain his business associates in the best style. He hadn't found her very sexy, but that really wasn't important. There was plenty of sex to be had in other directions, at any rate, there was in the circles in which he moved. Like any woman, Jenny had wanted children, and he'd given her three, in rapid tempo. The arrangement now was that she brought up the kids–his legitimate kids–she made the home attractive and respectable, and in return he gave her anything she wanted–clothes, a car, that sort of thing. He thought it worked very well.

Blanche White was one of the other directions. She was a pretty little thing of nineteen. She worked in one of Hadley's subsidiaries. Because she didn't read complex balance sheets, and because nobody told her, Blanche didn't realize that Hadley was her true boss. But she knew he was an important man, and she was flattered when he asked her to go out with him. She'd been out with him now quite a number of times, usually at intervals of two or three weeks. Hadley had taken her the second time, and he'd made her every time since. And now the silly little bitch had got herself in the family way. How was it possible to be so bloody stupid, he wondered. "Why were you so bloody stupid?" he asked her.

They were in the sitting room of a little place he'd had specially built, about five miles outside Nottingham. "I thought you, . . ." she began.

Hadley gave a snort and took a sharp snap of whiskey. "Don't be bloody daft. It's not up to men these days, not with all the new things they've got. Didn't anybody ever tell you?"

"I didn't like to go, to that clinic place."

"Didn't like to go! You'll like it a lot less, what's going to happen to you now!"

"What's to be done?" the girl sobbed.

"What's to be done! Stop being bloody daft, for one thing. See a doctor. Go on working as long as you can. Then I'll see you over it."

"See me over it!"

"What the hell else d'you expect? There's a hundred million kids born into the world every year. Don't think anybody's going to fall over backwards just because you're going to have one of 'em."

"Don't you care a bit?"

"I care a hell of a lot. D'you think it's any pleasure to me, this sort of thing? I'm not going to get anything out of it."

Hadley did get something out of it, much more than he could ever have imagined. He began with a small bonus. He took the little fool back to the bedroom. Tearfully, she let him do it again. He got far more out of it this second time than he expected in the circumstances. She again asked him, now in a whisper, to look after her. Once again, he told her he'd see she was all right. He left her there, thinking this was about as far as he could commit himself for the present. He took another sharp snap before starting back to Nottingham. He'd intended to stay here the night, told Jenny he'd be away the whole night. But he wasn't staying now, not with this situation to prey on his mind.

There was a stretch of some two miles of twisting country road before the main highway into Nottingham. He thought about Blanche White as he drove his big yellow Jaguar. She wouldn't give any trouble, too mouselike. He'd see her over it, like he said he would, until the kid was old enough to go to school. Then he'd find her a job. It might be worth his while to go on giving her a bit even after that. She'd only be twenty-three or twenty-four, useful in an emergency, perhaps.

The T-junction onto the highway came up. A vehicle was approaching from the left. It wasn't too far away, but far enough. Hadley saw no point in letting it get ahead of him. He gunned the big car as fiercely as he could. This was the time when it paid to have a piece of real machinery. The car leaped forward, straight into the track of the oncoming vehicle. Hadley took the turn at a bad angle. There was a blaze of light in his eyes, followed instantly by a blaze inside his head.

The other vehicle was driven by Jonathan Adams, forty-five, professor of philosophy at Oxford. He was on his way to Nottingham to give a lecture at the university there. He was to stay overnight with his opposite number, Jerome Renfrew. He knew Renfrew, of course, but not very well. This worried Adams, because he'd been delayed in leaving Oxford, so he would be arriving at the Renfrew household long after it was really proper for him to do so.

It was characteristic of Adams that he didn't know Renfrew very well, in fact, he didn't know anybody very well. A reticent, shy man, living in College rooms, what he liked most was travel, and reading, of course. Adams had a good reputation in his own field. He was a remarkably incisive lecturer for one so retiring in all other human contacts.

Adams was also a skillful driver. He'd batted along at a good pace all the way from Oxford, because he was so late, of course. Almost in Nottingham, he noticed the lights of a car moving along a side road ahead. It never crossed his mind that anybody could be fool enough to pull out into the main road, so he kept going ahead. Then, to his horror, the car did pull out, immediately in front of him. If only the fool had kept to the center of the road and left him with enough room to get through on the near side.

Jonathan Adams came to his senses still in the driver's seat. He sat there for a few moments. There was an instant when he was vaguely conscious of somebody peering into the car. He remembered leaving Oxford. He was driving to Nottingham, that was it. Then he remembered the side road and the other car, but he couldn't remember the actual collision. Still there must have been a collision, an appalling crash, unless at the last moment he'd managed only to sideswipe the other car. Perhaps he'd done that and then gone off the road, in which case it might not be too bad. Slowly, very gingerly, he tried moving his hands and arms. They were all right so far as he could tell, no sharp pain. Next the legs. They moved, so his spine wasn't dislocated. The head was now the critical thing. Gently he moved his hands upward over the face and skull. Not bad, so far as he could tell. It began to look as if he'd gone off the road with only a blow hard enough to put him out for a few moments. He decided to risk it, to try climbing out of the car. He knew he shouldn't do this, really. Better to wait for an ambulance. Some passing driver would be sure to call the police. There might be internal injuries. The temptation was too strong, however, to be out of this coffin-like box in which he seemed to be entombed. It was a difficult business, for the car had been knocked onto its side. He saw now why he'd felt so queer, because he hadn't been sitting upright. After a struggle he managed it. Miraculously he was standing there looking down at the wreckage. It looked pretty bad, not much worth salvaging.

A man came up to him and said, "What the bloody hell d'you mean by coming along at that speed?"

"Did you see the collision?"

"Did I see it, of course I saw it. I'm the driver of the other bloody car."

"Then we'd better exchange insurance companies."

"You're damn right we'd better. That was a valuable car of mine. Not much but scrap there now."

"You did come out of the side road, you know."

Adams knew it was better not to argue. Leave things for the police to judge. The reply convinced him of this. "Don't give me that story. There was plenty of time to get out into the road, if you hadn't been driving like a flaming maniac. Right into the back of my car, bloody well into the bloody backside, right up its arse. You'll see what they do to you for that."

Adams also knew he really should have slowed down a bit. After all, nobody was better aware than he of how full the world was with fools. Even so, it was hard luck to have picked such a prize specimen.

"Better give me your insurance card, or your name. Here's

mine," he said, handing over the insurance certificate he always carried in his wallet.

"Think you're going to get mine, do you?"

"Unless I do, the police will know exactly what to think."

"You poor fish, you poor, bloody fish. What makes you think I haven't got the police *and* the magistrates all sewn up around here?"

"You may have them sewn up, but I can assure you Counsel from London will very soon unsew them."

At this Hadley realized he'd been unlucky. He'd drawn an educated man who wouldn't be put down. It didn't really matter, of course, only the no-claim bonus. It was just that he didn't like to be beaten, to be shown up to be in the wrong. He would have paid out a hundred no-claim bonuses just to be able to fix this little bugger. However, he realized he'd better turn over his name and address: Arthur Hadley, "The Gables," Arntree Road, Nottingham.

The flashing blue light of a police car could be seen approaching from the direction of Nottingham. Behind the police car was an ambulance. Both vehicles drew to a halt by the side of the road. Out of one came two policemen, out of the other two attendants with a stretcher. Adams was at first surprised. Then he remembered his impression of somebody peering into his car, a passing motorist who had obviously called the police. He walked toward the attendants. It would be best to get them to drive him to the Renfrew household–at least now he would have a good excuse for being late. The Hadley man, he knew, would be tackling the police. Let the fool talk to them as much as he wanted. God, what a bore the fellow was. The police would come to him for his story all in good time, better when he was rested than now. The thing to do was to get to bed as soon as possible. There was certain to be some delayed shock.

Adams stepped up to the nearest ambulance man and said, "Luckily neither of us is badly hurt, a few bruises, perhaps. I wonder if you'd be kind enough to take me into Nottingham?"

The man was walking toward him, his companion behind, as they carried the stretcher. Neither of them paused in the slightest degree. The rear man came so close that Adams felt the fellow must surely brush against him. Yet he felt not the slightest contact. Hadley came rushing up, "Can't make the buggers hear. Not a bloody word. What's going on?"

"I don't know, but why don't you shut up? Stop the verbal diarrhea just for a couple of minutes."

This kept Hadley quiet, more or less, for a little while.

The policemen and the attendants conferred together. Adams heard one of them say, "Looks bad," then another added, "This sort of thing always gets me in the pit of the stomach." Then the four men busied themselves in the wreckage. Adams watched as something was lifted, presumably a body, into the ambulance. "Funny, there's only one corpse," he heard an attendant say to one of the policemen, "where's the other one gone?"

Hadley could take it no longer. He strode up to the four men and shouted, "Stop this fooling, you silly buggers. Can't you see we're here. We're all right. There's nothing wrong with us. What you need is your bloody lugs cleaning out."

This outburst produced not the slightest response. Hysterically desperate now, Hadley rushed at the nearest man. There was no effect, no contact. Then Hadley broke down. Alternately, he whined and roared and jabbered, nothing but gibberish. Then he stopped and began to shiver violently.

The ambulance men searched around again and then drove away. There was nothing Jonathan Adams could do to stop them. The policemen stayed around for quite a while longer, making extensive notes. When they drove off there was nothing that could be done to stop them either.

"You'd think they were a lot of muckering ghosts, the way they're going on," said Hadley.

"When you say ghosts, I think you're not very wide of the mark. Except it's exactly the other way round."

"You mean we're ghosts?"

"Yes. Doesn't it strike you as queer we're both of us pretty well unhurt? I hardly seem to be bruised."

Hadley became much calmer.

"What's to be bloody well done about it?"

"I don't know. The strange thing is they seemed to have one body in the ambulance. Did you have a passenger in your car?"

Hadley wondered if by any chance Blanche White had sneaked into his car. Then he realized she couldn't have. He'd left her in a state of undress, as the newspapers put it, in the big bed out at his place. "No, I didn't. What about you?"

"I'd hardly have asked the question if I'd had a passenger, would I?"

The two of them began to walk along the road toward Nottingham. A number of cars passed by. They walked on for half an hour or so when Hadley asked, "Did you see that body?"

"No. I tried to, but somehow the light was never right."

"Whose body d'you think it was?"

"One of us."

"How the hell could it be?"

"I don't know. If it wasn't one of us, who else was it?"

"There should have been two bodies."

"You'd certainly think so."

"Could the other one have got minced up, into pieces?"

"I doubt it. That's what they were looking for."

"Where were you going to in Nottingham?"

"To stay with an acquaintance."

"He's not going to put out the bloody welcome mat now, is he?"

"Hardly. You know, the curious thing to me is the road is just as hard as it always was and the wind is just as cold. Quite nippy, in fact. I suppose I'd better go to a hotel. At least there shouldn't be any difficulty about getting in, not if they can't hear me or see me."

"Hell to that. You'd better come home with me. See if we

can stir up the wife. Told her I'd be away tonight. Actually, I was intending to spend it with a douce."

"A what?"

"A douce, a bird, a female. Out at a little shack I've got in the country."

"But you didn't."

"No, something cropped up. Anyway, we'll see what the little wifie's got to say."

It was about two-thirty A.M. when the two men arrived at "The Gables." Hadley let them in with his key. To his surprise, the lights were all on, everywhere.

"Funny, I didn't notice the lights when we were outside."

"Nor did I."

They went out again, and sure enough the house was in darkness. Inside again, the lights were on. Hadley tried flicking the switches. It made no difference, the lights stayed on.

Hadley went off upstairs to see if he could get any response from Jennifer. Within seconds, Adams heard him roaring and ranting. It went on for a couple of minutes or so. Then Hadley appeared at the top of the stairs and shouted down, "Hey, come up here a minute."

Adams trotted up the two flights. At the top Hadley took him by the arm and literally ran into a large bedroom. Like everywhere else, the light was burning. In the bed was a brunette with a fair-haired young man, both sound asleep. "Look at that, just look at that, look at the bloody bitch," shrieked Hadley.

Adams surmised this must be the "wifie." She had a bare arm out across the bedclothes. Her hair was streaming over the pillow. It was impossible to mistake the languid, satisfied expression on the woman's face, even in sleep. Hadley rushed furiously at the bed, snatching at the blankets, with the evident intention of ripping the covers off the pair of them. Once again, there was no contact. Further roaring and ranting was of no avail.

Adams began to get sleepy, which meant he was getting

bored. But then the woman turned in her sleep. The hair moved and tickled the young man into wakefulness.

"Now listen to me, you bastard," roared Hadley, "I'm going to thrash you within an inch of your life." Hadley picked up a bedside lamp and crashed it down on the young man's head. There was quite an amount of glass in the lamp. It shattered violently against the wall, but the young man neither heard the noise nor felt the blow. He began to caress the woman into wakefulness. "Not again, Mike!" she murmured. The two moved closer and closer; meanwhile, Hadley flung down on their heads a veritable cascade of bedroom articles. Not a jot or a tittle of difference did it make. The love-making went ahead without letup or hindrance. Jonathan Adams, being a shy man, moved out of the bedroom. Then his duty as a professional philosopher asserted itself, for how could he forsake the singular situation now developing to its climax? If ever he came to write his Principia, this must surely find a scholarly place within its cover.

At the end, the woman stretched herself luxuriously and said, "How much more delectable than my old goat of a husband can provide."

Hadley was now screaming and raging like a maniac. To Jonathan Adams' view, the bedroom was littered with wreckage. Yet the two in the bed noticed nothing at all. Apparently weary but sublimely contented, they fell asleep again. Adams too was sleepy now. He found his way to another bedroom and laid himself down. His last sensation before sleep claimed him was of a distant rumbling, as Hadley still sought vainly to attract the attention of his errant wife and of her young lover, Mike Johnson.

Blanche White woke with the first light. She had passed a disturbed night in the big bed, weeping from time to time into the linen pillowslips, and stubbing her toes against the incongruous eighteenth-century furniture when she had made an expedition to the bathroom. As the girl dressed slowly, a new resolution came to her. It had no great determination at the back of it, but at least it was a moment of firmness, more than Blanche White had ever shown before. She decided to go and have it out with Arthur's wife. The woman was said to be a snooty piece, but she'd stand up for her rights now, Blanche decided, even if it meant a first-class bust-up. Her ideas were all confused as to what her rights were and of exactly where the wife came into it. The one thing clear to the girl was that she couldn't be treated in quite this casual style. If Arthur hadn't taken her back to the big bed for a second time last night, she might have felt like putting up with it all. But it couldn't be right, for him always to be treating her the way he wanted to do, as if her feelings didn't matter at all.

So Blanche White walked the two miles to the main road. There she caught an early workman's bus into the city. It was coming up to eight A.M. by the time she reached The Gables. She found Mrs. Hadley just coming down to breakfast. To her intense surprise, she found a young man there as well.

Jennifer, Mike Johnson, and Blanche White sat around the breakfast table and talked. Unseen and unheard, Arthur Hadley and Jonathan Adams sat there beside them, listening to the excited conversation. "We've got him good and proper this time, a clean, straightforward divorce, a big settlement *and* custody of the children."

Johnson turned to Blanche White. "It all depends on you, Blanche. Stand firm and we've got him by the short hairs. This is the way to fix the old bastard."

"That's just where you're bloody well wrong," bellowed Hadley. "What I'll give her will make your lousy money look like a penny piece compared to a five-pound note. I'll buy her, lock, stock, and barrel. It's you who'll be in the divorce box, not me. By God, I'll roast the vitals out of you, Jenny."

Not a word did they hear. The plans went forward step by step, detail by detail, until there was a loud knock on the hall door. Johnson was upstairs in a flash. Blanche answered the door. It was a police sergeant to see Mrs. Hadley.

Blanche showed the sergeant into the large, spacious lounge.

A moment later, after a whispered conversation, Jennifer joined the sergeant. Hadley and Adams also went into the lounge, quite unseen.

"Mrs. Hadley?"

"Yes, I'm Mrs. Hadley."

"I'm afraid I've got bad news, Mrs. Hadley."

Jennifer waited, and the sergeant went on, "It's your husband. His car was involved in an accident last night, at approximately one in the morning."

"But what happened to *him?* I'm not interested in the car."

The sergeant shifted uneasily, "We don't really know. That's why I'm here. You see, two cars were involved in a collision. But only one of the drivers was found there when an ambulance got to the spot. We think the other driver must have taken a blow on the head and must have gone wandering off somewhere. It sometimes happens in these accident cases."

"Yes, I understand that. But *who* is it that was injured?"

"Dead, I'm afraid, Mrs. Hadley. We don't know. That's just the point. We'd like you to come down and make an identification. That is to say, if it *is* Mr. Hadley. We've got someone else coming in to check on the other party."

"Surely you can tell from the position where the body was found? You know which was my husband's car."

"We know that. But the cars came together, so that they sort of stuck together. It wasn't clear just what had happened."

Shortly after, the sergeant took his leave.

The three, Jennifer, Mike Johnson, and Blanche White discussed this new turn of events. Then Jennifer said, "How soon d'you think we ought to go?"

"Right away. There's no point in delay, best to get it over with."

"Mike, I'd rather like to have one of Arthur's business partners there. So we can talk to him afterwards, in case it happens to be Arthur. I think I'll call Tony. Suppose you get the car ready."

Jennifer went off to make the telephone call.

Jonathan Adams walked out of the spacious lounge and out of the front door of The Gables. Hadley ran after him shouting, "Where the hell are you going?"

"The morgue. This will give us a chance to find out what's really under that sheet. We'll have to hurry if we're to get there in time. Maybe you don't want to come?"

But Hadley decided he would come. Then he wanted to know why they must walk, why they couldn't ride in the car. "Try it if you like, but I think you'll find there's no contact."

On the way into the city, Adams remarked, "I believe I've got it straight at last. One of us is going to be under that sheet, dead. The other is going to be found wandering around the countryside, alive."

"I don't bloody well understand."

"I think it isn't decided yet, whether it's to be you or me."

"How d'you mean?"

"It's going to depend on what they want."

"Who?"

"All of them, of course, when they get there, to the morgue."

The walk into the city went by very quickly, faster than Hadley could ever remember it. Hadley wasn't quite sure of exactly which building the morgue was in. But he knew the right street, so they simply waited for Jennifer, Mike Johnson, and Blanche White to arrive and followed after them. A police constable escorted the party into a waiting room, where they found the sergeant again. Another man, whom Adams recognized as Jerome Renfrew, was also there. The sergeant made the introductions and then said, "I've had a telephone message from Sir Anthony Brown. He says he'll be here in a few moments. We'll wait for him if you're agreeable."

True to his word, Sir Anthony appeared at about nine-thirty A.M. He was well-tailored, spruce, very nearly in complete contrast to Hadley in every respect.

The sergeant accompanied them into the morgue. Adams heard the clack-clack of their shoes on the hard floor. He expected it would all be over in a flash. The sheet would be whipped away, the decision would irretrievably be made, life or death for him–and death or life for Hadley. No doubt this was what really took place. No doubt the sheet was indeed whipped quickly away. Yet this was not the way it appeared to Adams or to Hadley. The action seemed to stop, as if all the world had stopped, as if an infinity of time was available for past actions to be considered and for human problems to be thought through.

There were five of them: Sir Anthony Brown, Jerome Renfrew, Jennifer Hadley, Mike Johnson, and Blanche White. Adams saw there must be a decision. Surely it must be a vote, nothing else was possible, for there could hardly be unanimity among these five–unanimity as to who they wanted dead and who they wanted alive. Adams was worried he would never know how each person voted. They would hardly speak their innermost thoughts aloud. Then, to his astonishment, he found he could hear those thoughts, he could hear them as each of the five came in turn to a decision. Hadley could hear them, too. Hadley knew what the real issue was now, it all showed in the strained, terrified look on his face.

Sir Anthony Brown was the first. To him there was no issue: "I'll be ruined if it's Hadley. The bastard has spread everything too thin, we're at full stretch. Perhaps Hadley could pull us through, with all his contacts. I'm certain I can't. Please to God it isn't Hadley."

Score: Hadley 1, Adams 0.

Hadley bellowed at the top of his voice, "Good old yellow-bellied Tony. He knows on which side *his* bread's buttered."

Then Jerome Renfrew came up: "I wonder who'll get Adams' chair if it's him. Of course, I can't hope it's Adams, not because of his chair. I believe Hadley has a rather unsavory reputation, with young girls of Sally's age. I can't say I *hope* it's Hadley, but of course I'd prefer it to be Hadley."

Score: Hadley 1, Adams 1.

"Bugger," yelled Hadley, sweat on his face now. "One thing I'll promise you, you bloody fancy-panty, that daughter of yours, that Sally, I'll have her on her back if it costs me a million quid."

The real drama started with Jennifer Hadley: "God, what a relief it would be to have him gone, to be free from such a lousy bully."

Instantly, Hadley was on his knees, whining, "No, Jenny, no, don't go against me. I'll give you anything, Mike Johnson, if you like. You can have him every night, every day, if you want. In Christ's name, don't kill me, Jenny."

Quite unaffected by this outburst, Jennifer Hadley went on: "I wonder if Tony's right. He told me on the phone this morning, the business is certain to go to pieces without Arthur. I haven't any real property of my own. I'll get a share in Arthur's estate, of course, but that wouldn't be much good if the estate went bankrupt. I suppose I might even be responsible for the debts. I couldn't face being penniless, not with three young children. The divorce we were talking about this morning really looks much much safer. I'd be just as free from Arthur that way. Of course, it's pretty rotten to prefer it to be some innocent man instead of Arthur, but nobody could blame me for preferring it not to be my husband."

Score: Hadley 2, Adams 1.

Then Mike Johnson: "It seems pretty awful to think this way, but if it's Hadley, I'll get Jenny, I'll get everything, the lot. Not that I don't enjoy sleeping with her, just for its own sake. But after all, she is a few years older than me. And I'd have to put up with Hadley's children. I wouldn't like 'em to take after the father, especially the boy. So it's pretty fair, to get some compensation. Of course, there's the divorce, but that's really very chancey. Hadley will do his best to buy off the White girl. So the divorce might not work. This way it's one hundred percent certain. Besides, I'm sick to the back teeth with Hadley's foul mouth and temper."

Score: Hadley 2, Adams 2.

At this, Hadley broke into a hysterical frenzy, perspiration streaming down his face and his body. His shirt showed a dozen or more large wet patches. Jonathan Adams spoke for the first time, "Can you not be quiet, man, even when you are but a hairsbreadth from death?"

It all depended on Blanche White, the girl Hadley treated with such callous disregard. She had stood there longer than any of the others, turning things over and over in her mind. She knew nothing of Adams. It never occurred to her that she was deciding between Hadley and a man of quite an opposite temper, that Adams would hardly have dared to ask her to go out with him, that if he had–if by some miracle Adams had conquered his shyness and had done to her what Hadley had done–Adams would have stood by her fully and completely. She knew nothing of this, she knew only of her own plight: "If he's dead, there can't be a divorce. So his wife won't need me. She'll have lots, of course, because she's his wife. But she won't help me, she'll just laugh and say I was a fool, the same as he did. He wouldn't help me much, but he'd see I was all right. That's what he said, he'd see I was all right. He'll help me because it's his kid, that's why. Oh, God, I hope it's not him."

Score: Hadley 3, Adams 2.

The sergeant whipped away the sheet from the corpse. The bruised body of Jonathan Adams lay there on the slab. During the mid-morning, Arthur Hadley was found wandering in fields about two miles from the place of the accident. Reconstruction showed Adams to have taken the full force of the collision, coming in as he did from behind. Hadley was hit hard, but with the protection of the steering wheel in front and of the bulk of a heavy car behind, he suffered only comparatively minor injuries. After a couple of days, his memory returned to the point when he had left Blanche White, out at his special place in the country. He was never able to recover anything further than this.

Superficially, it might seem from the geometry of the accident as if it must inevitably have been Adams who was killed, Hadley who survived. This simple-minded interpretation takes no account of the possibility that Adams might have cut his car still further in on the near side. Had he done so, the two cars would have locked together, spun off the road, and come to rest as the front of Hadley's car crashed against a tree. The decision rested on Adams, on his split-second reaction to Hadley's car blundering in front of him. Now, Adams' split-second reaction depended on electronic neurological activity in his brain, which in the last analysis turned on a single quantum event, on whether the event took place or not. Until the winding sheet was whipped away from the body in the morgue, the wave function representing the event was still in what physicists call a "mixed state." Let it be added, for the sake of the smart physicist, that a clue to the solution of the deepest problem of theoretical physics—the condensation of the Schroedinger wave function—is to be found in the manner in which our jury of five arrived at their decision.

In the sequel, Hadley just managed to keep his businesses on an even keel. Jennifer tried unsuccessfully for a divorce. Hadley paid Blanche White well enough for the girl to keep her mouth shut. It wasn't the first time he'd had to pay out, and it wouldn't be the last. What the hell did it matter, really, a few quid? Mike Johnson was sent as manager of the new business at Sheffield. This more or less terminated his affair with Jennifer, although there were rare meetings between them which sputtered on for a year or two.

During the final scene in the morgue, it had at last become clear to Adams, a gentle, rather brave man, exactly where his life had gone wrong. Adams was a man who felt commitments so deeply that he hesitated to make any at all. It was because he felt even a mild commitment to a woman implied a complete commitment that he had remained a bachelor. Just because he felt he must give a great deal if he gave at all, life had passed him by. He was without connections anywhere, if one excepts the trivia of everyday life in his Oxford College.

Hadley was the exact opposite. He accepted the deepest of commitments and then gave little when he should have given much. But Hadley did give a little, which was why, goat and lousy bully that he was, the vote fell to him.

It may be thought the vote an unfair one, taken in Hadley's territory. But Adams had no territory for the vote to be taken in. Moreover, Adams started with a vote in hand, since it was hardly conceivable for Renfrew to make his choice in any other way. Adams only needed to split Hadley's territory down the middle to give himself a three-to-two victory. Everyone in Hadley's territory voted sharply in their own self-interest. Only Renfrew's vote was altruistic, for in truth Renfrew was himself a strong candidate for Adams' chair.

In one of his finest passages, Rabelais advises us all to become debtors. As the debtor grows older, the whole world wishes him well, the great man points out, for only if the debtor stays alive can his creditors have any hope of recovering their lendings. As a rich man grows older, the world gathers around, waiting for him to die, as a group of vultures might gather to plan the distribution of his flesh before the last breath was out of his body. The same truth applies more deeply than even Rabelais saw. It applies at the deepest levels of emotion. Adams was the creditor, Hadley the debtor.

BLACKMAIL

Angus Carruthers was a wayward, impish genius. Genius is not the same thing as high ability. Men of great talent commonly spread their efforts, often very effectively, over a wide front. The true genius devotes the whole of his skill, his energies, his intelligence, to a particular objective, which he pursues unrelentingly.

Early in life, Carruthers became skeptical of human superiority over other animals. Already in his early teens, he understood exactly where the difference lies–it lies in the ability of humans to pool their knowledge through speech, in the ability through speech to educate the young. The challenging problem to his keen mind was to find a system of communication every bit as powerful as language that could be made available to others of the higher animals. The basic idea was not original, it was the determination to carry the idea through to its conclusion that was new. Carruthers pursued his objective inflexibly down the years.

Gussie had no patience with people who talked and chattered to animals. If animals had the capacity to understand language, wouldn't they have done it already, he said, thousands of years ago? Talk was utterly and completely pointless. You were just damned stupid if you thought you were going to teach English to your pet dog or cat. The thing to do was to understand the world from the point of view of the dog or cat. Once you'd got yourself into *their* system, it would be time enough to think about trying to get them into *your* system.

Gussie had no close friends. I suppose I was about as near to being a friend as anyone, yet even I would see him only perhaps once in six months. There was always something refreshingly different when you happened to run into him. He might have grown a black spade beard, or he might just have had a crewcut. He might be wearing a flowing cape, or he might be neatly tailored in a Bond Street suit. He always trusted me well enough to show off his latest experiments. At the least they were remarkable, at the best they went far beyond anything I had heard of, or read about. To my repeated suggestions that he simply must "publish," he always responded with a long, wheezy laugh. To me it seemed just plain common sense to publish, if only to raise money for the experiments, but Gussie obviously didn't see it this way. How he managed for money I could never discover. I supposed him to have a private income, which was very likely correct.

One day I received a note asking me to proceed to such-and-such an address, sometime near four P.M. on a certain Saturday. There was nothing unusual in my receiving a note, for Carruthers had got in touch with me several times before in this way. It was the address which came as the surprise, a house in a Croydon suburb. On previous occasions, I had always gone out to some decrepit barn of a place in remotest

Hertfordshire. The idea of Gussie in Croydon somehow didn't fit. I was sufficiently intrigued to put off a previous appointment and to hie myself along at the appropriate hour.

My wild notion that Carruthers might have got himself well and truly wed, that he might have settled down in a nine-to-five job, turned out to be quite wrong. The big tortoise-shell spectacles he had sported at our previous meeting were gone, replaced by plain steel rims. His lank black hair was medium-long this time. He had a lugubrious look about him, as if he had just been rehearsing the part of Quince in *A Midsummer Night's Dream.*

"Come in," he wheezed.

"What's the idea, living in these parts?" I asked as I slipped off my overcoat. For answer, he broke into a whistling, croaking laugh. "Better take a look, in there."

The door to which Gussie pointed was closed. I was pretty sure I would find animals "in there," and so it proved. Although the room was darkened by a drawn curtain, there was sufficient light for me to see three creatures crouched around a television set. They were intently watching the second half of a game of Rugby League football. There was a cat with a big rust-red patch on the top of its head. There was a poodle, which cocked an eye at me for a fleeting second as I went in, and there was a furry animal sprawled in a big armchair. As I went in, I had the odd impression of the animal lifting a paw, as if by way of greeting. Then I realized it was a small brown bear.

I had known Gussie long enough now, I had seen enough of his work, to realize that any comment in words would be ridiculous and superfluous. I had long ago learned the right procedure, to do exactly the same thing as the animals themselves were doing. Since I have always been partial to rugby, I was able to settle down quite naturally to watch the game in company with this amazing trio. Every so often I found myself catching the bright, alert eyes of the bear. I soon realized that, whereas I was mainly interested in the run of the ball, the animals were mainly interested in the tackling, qua tackling. Once, when a player was brought down particularly heavily, there was a muffled yap from the poodle, instantly answered by a grunt from the bear.

After perhaps twenty minutes, I was startled by a really loud bark from the dog, there being nothing at all in the game to warrant such an outburst. Evidently the dog wanted to attract the attention of the engrossed bear, for when the bear looked up quizzically, the dog pointed a dramatic paw toward a clock standing a couple of yards to the left of the television set. Immediately the bear lumbered from its chair to the set. It fumbled with the controls. There was a click, and to my astonishment we were on another channel. A wrestling bout had just begun.

The bear rolled back to its chair. It stretched itself, resting lazily on the base of its spine, arms raised with the claws cupped behind the head. One of the wrestlers spun the other violently. There was a loud thwack as the unfortunate fellow cracked his head on a ring post. At this, the cat let out the strangest animal noise I had ever heard. Then it settled down into a deep, powerful purr.

I had seen and heard enough. As I quitted the room the bear waved me out, much in the style of royalty and visiting heads of state. I found Gussie placidly drinking tea in what was evidently the main sitting room of the house. To my frenzied requests to be told exactly what it meant, Gussie responded with his usual asthmatic laugh. Instead of answering my questions, he asked some of his own. "I want your advice, professionally, as a lawyer. There's nothing illegal in the animals watching television, is there? Or in the bear switching the programs?"

"How could there be?"

"The situation's a bit complicated. Here, take a look at this."

Carruthers handed me a typewritten list. It covered a week of television programs. If this represented viewing by the animals, the set must have been switched on more or less continuously. The programs were all of one type, sports, Westerns, suspense plays, films of violence.

"What they love," said Gussie by way of explanation, "is the sight of humans bashing themselves to pieces. Really, of course, it's more or less the usual popular taste, only a bit more so."

I noticed the name of a well-known rating firm on the letterhead.

"What's this heading here? I mean, what's all this to do with the T.V. ratings?"

Gussie fizzed and crackled like a soda siphon. "That's exactly the point. This house here is one of the odd few hundreds used in compiling the weekly ratings. That's why I asked if there was anything wrong in Bingo doing the switching."

"You don't mean viewing by those animals is going into the ratings?"

"Not only here, but in three other houses I've bought. I've got a team of chaps in each of them. Bears take quite naturally to the switching business."

"There'll be merry hell to pay if it comes out. Can't you see what the papers will make of it?"

"Very clearly, indeed."

The point hit me at last. Gussie could hardly have come on four houses by chance, all of which just happened to be hooked up to the T.V. rating-system. As far as I could see, there wasn't anything illegal in what he'd done, so long as he didn't make any threats or demands. As if he read my thoughts, he pushed a slip of paper under my nose. It was a check for fifty thousand pounds.

"Unsolicited," he wheezed, "came out of the blue. From somebody in the advertising game, I suppose. Hush money. The problem is, do I put myself in the wrong if I cash it?"

Before I could form an opinion on this tricky question, there came a tinkling of breaking glass. "Another one gone," Gussie muttered. "I haven't been able to teach Bingo to use the vertical or horizontal holds. Whenever anything goes wrong, or the program goes off for a minute, he hammers away at the thing. It's always the tube that goes."

"It must be a costly business."

"Averages about a dozen a week. I always keep a spare set ready. Be a good fellow and give me a hand with it. They'll get pretty shirty if we don't move smartly."

We lifted what seemed like a brand-new set from out of a cupboard. Each gripping an end of it, we edged our way to the television snuggery. From inside, I was now aware of a strident uproar, compounded from the bark of a dog, the grunt of a bear, and the shrill moan of a red-headed cat. It was the uproar of animals suddenly denied their intellectual pabulum.

ELEMENT 79

The cosmic powers, the inner powers, you understand, like a good lotus-eater when they see one. They had some rare beauties on their hands now. Yet the inner powers do not like breaking the natural order of things too flagrantly, although they're not above slipping in what mathematicians are pleased to call a perturbation. This time they were willing to interfere to the extent of slipping in a chip of rock the size of a pea.

Some four and a half billion years ago the inner planets were formed by condensation in a gas cloud that quitted the Sun for dynamical reasons. The gas was pushed further and further away. As it moved outward, solid and liquid particles were formed, common refractory materials first, then less common, less refractory materials. Innermost were common metals and rock, composed mainly of elements 8, 12, 14, and 26—iron, that is to say, and the oxides of magnesium and silicon.

Element 79 is almost as refractory as iron, but it was present in the gas in very much smaller quantity. The vapor pressure was much much lower than the vapor pressure of iron. So element 79 didn't condense until the gases moved considerably further away from the Sun. Whereas the ordinary metals and the rock were precipitated mainly in the region of Venus and Earth, element 79 did not condense until the gases reached the region between Mars and Jupiter. In fact, element 79 was precipitated in the asteroidal belt. A thermodynamic calculation will show how very sensitive the condensation process was to distance from the Sun. (*Nota bene:* Because of the very small vapor pressure, the temperature had to be rather low, about 750K, compared to 1500K for iron. This meant that the well-known exponential factor involving the binding energy of the atoms into the solid crystal lattice was a very large number, the factor of the form exp Q/kT. This, in turn, meant the condensation was very temperature-sensitive, and hence sensitive to distance from the Sun.)

The significance of these technicalities is that condensation of element 79 was a quite critical process. Scarcely any of it condensed before the gases reached a certain distance, actually 2.257 ··· A.U., then all of it suddenly dropped out of the vapor into solid objects, which were of almost pure element 79. The objects were mostly about one or two tenths of a kilometer in radius and there were about a thousand of them. It was on these objects that the cosmic powers, the inner powers, concentrated their attention for a brief instant.

What they intended was to bring one of the objects close to Mars at exactly the right place and time. It was natural to choose the particular object that came nearest to fulfilling their requirements in the ordinary way of things. Then a calculation was performed in the following way. All the particles in the asteroidal belt were numbered. There were many millions of them. Then quantities $I(r/s/t/\cdots)$ were worked out for all combinations of values of r, s, t, ··· The meaning of these quantities was quite simple. For instance, by $I(r/s/t)$ is meant the impulse that had to be given to the rth asteroidal particle in order for it to hit the sth particle, which in turn would hit the tth particle, which in turn would hit the required object in exactly the right way to bring it near to Mars at the right time and place. By $I(r/s/t/u)$ is similarly meant the impulse that had to be given to the rth particle in order for it to hit the sth particle, in order for it to hit the tth particle, in order for it to hit the uth particle, which would then hit the required object in exactly the required way. Similarly, too, for still more complicated combinations, like $I(r/s/t/u/u)$. In this game of cosmic billiards the calculations were kept going until an impulse was obtained that could be achieved by placing the prescribed chip of rock the size of a pea at a precisely defined spot at a precisely defined time. It will be clear that the calculations had to be done not only for all combinations of the asteroidal particles but for different moments of time. This was why the sheer volume of the calculations was far beyond human capability.

The fateful chip of rock was slipped into position. A meteorite a foot in diameter hit it a glancing blow. The resulting modification in the orbit of the meteorite was quite minute. Yet by the end of the year it was sufficient to change the position of the meteorite by more than fifty miles, sufficient to cause it to hit, slap-bang, another meteorite, this time about ten yards in diameter. The same pattern was repeated for a whole chain of particles until at last a rather large one plugged its way into the object composed of essentially pure element 79.

The perihelion distance of the object–its closest distance to the Sun, that is to say–was now almost exactly the same as the mean radius of the orbit of Mars. In the ordinary way of things, a close approach between the object and Mars was to be expected sooner or later. The approach came sooner, because the calculations had been exactly performed. The approach was close, the object almost shaved the surface of

Mars. It approached Mars more or less along the line of the motion of Mars about the Sun, and its speed of approach relative to the planet was a little less than 2.3 kilometers per second.

The object accelerated as it came in, due to the gravitational pull of the planet. It had some 5.5 kilometers per second at its nearest point. It tore its way through the thin atmosphere of Mars. The scouring effect of the atmospheric gases did no harm. In fact, quite the reverse. The dirt deposited on the surface of the object throughout the eons was simply removed. It now had a rich, warm, yellow color.

As seen by an observer sited on Mars, the object would have appeared to recede with almost exactly the same speed as it had come, 2.3 kilometers per second. However, the direction of recession was quite different from that of the approach; it was switched by almost a right angle. Whereas the object had come in along the direction of orbital motion, it now went out along a line drawn from the Sun to Mars. The orbit around the Sun was changed again, of course. Instead of going back to the original position in the asteroidal belt, the object simply oscillated about the orbit of Mars itself. In fact, Mars and the object had very similar orbits, which meant that a further encounter between them was inevitable.

A second very close approach occurred some three years later. The second approach was rather like a mirror-image version of the first approach. Once more the direction of motion of the object was switched essentially through a right angle—this as seen from Mars again. The approach was along the line from Mars to the Sun, the recession was in a direction *opposite* to the orbital motion of Mars about the Sun. The switch involved points of very real subtlety. It involved the object sweeping around the *morning* side of the planet–if it had swept around the *evening* side the object would have gone more or less back to the asteroidal belt. Now it lost still more angular momentum, so the new orbit had to dip well inside that of Mars.

In fact, the new orbit dipped as far in as the Earth. Encounters with the Earth were now to be expected. In the ordinary way of things it might have needed a hundred thousand years or more before an actual collision occurred. Here there was a precisely calculated situation, however. Inexorably, under the exact law of gravitation, the object followed a trajectory aimed at the Earth. It was incredibly accurate shooting. The Earth was a bull's-eye target, occupying only one-millionth part of the total target area.

As the object came in close, it looked for a while as if the encounter was going to be a near miss. But at the last moment the Earth's gravitational field caused the object to come in a little closer. It plunged into the atmosphere and hit the terrestrial surface at nearly a grazing angle on the night side. It was as if a bullet had just nicked the very edge of the bull's-eye. Yet there was no mistake here, no small error of calculation. It had to be just that way, for the following reason.

The object came to the Earth nearly along the line of the Earth's motion about the Sun. It overtook the Earth, having an orbital speed in excess of the Earth by a little over 3 kilometers per second. As it came closer, the Earth's pull on it increased the speed. By the time the object hit the atmosphere, it was moving relative to the Earth at more than 11 kilometers per second. Now this is far above the speed of sound in a solid crystal of element 79. A direct head-on collision between the object and the Earth would have gasified the object. Essentially the whole of the element 79 would have gone into the terrestrial atmosphere. It would have been largely irrecoverable. Indeed, the whole enterprise would have been utterly wasted. With a grazing collision things were different. Here one had to compare, not the 11 kilometers per second with the speed of sound in the solid crystal of element 79, but the 11 kilometers per second multiplied by the sine of the grazing angle. That is to say, one had to compare the normal component of the collision speed with the sound speed. At a sufficiently small grazing angle the sound speed would be bigger. Then the object would not be gasified. It would behave more like a huge drop of liquid. It would burst into a multitude of small fragments.

The object was about one third of a kilometer in diameter. Some of it evaporated away at the surface as it came in through the terrestrial atmosphere, but only a little. The total mass was of order 3.10^{14} grams. With each gram possessing a kinetic energy near 5.10^{11} ergs, the total energy released on impact was more than 10^{26} ergs. The effect was much like a great earthquake, not at all the sort of thing that security services could keep secret.

When you consider the boom generated by an airplane, say of mass 10^9 grams, moving at a speed of less than 1 kilometer per second, particularly when you consider that the boom increases as a high power of the speed, the sonic effect of the object can hardly be imagined. It came in over the British Isles from the Atlantic like the clappers of hell.

In the track of the object the temperature was lifted to 30,000C. Most of the energy communicated to the atmospheric gases was dissipated as radiation. The radiative flash was as bright as the Sun and it lasted for several minutes, long after the actual impact.

The point of impact lay in a big area of desolate country, in the Monadhliath Mountains to the north of Newtonmore and Kingussie. Devastation spread out in all directions, reaching even to the south of Edinburgh and Glasgow. The first impression was of a national disaster. Then, more accurately, of a Scottish disaster. Damage was estimated to exceed five thousand million pounds.

It was some days before the first survey party got into the area. The members were astonished to find an incredible profusion of nuggets of a warm, yellowish metal. In size the debris ranged from little droplets a few millimeters in diameter up to great chunks the size of your fist. They were found scattered everywhere over an area of a hundred square miles. Within a few hours, a simple chemical analysis revealed element 79, worth, at the current stabilized world price, about one and one-half dollars per gram.

The government acted instantly. A sequence of barriers operated by the military were set up. The outer cordon prevented the average citizen to the south from entering the Highlands at all. Inner barriers stopped you from getting close to the critical area. Since all the roads were dreadfully damaged, ordinary transportation was in any case impossible. Only vehicles with a caterpillar drive could move about with any freedom.

The cleaning-up operation took a long time. It was the best part of a year before all the metal was safely under lock and key, in enormous vaults newly constructed at a dozen different locations throughout the south of England. The government would very much have liked to keep the whole operation secret. But this was quite impossible. Enough of the metal had got itself into private hands for the chemical nature of the object to have become known throughout the world. What nobody knew, however, outside the government, was the quantity of metal. Rumor said there was a tremendous lot of it, but even rumor grossly underestimated the situation. There was 3.10^{14} grams of it, worth five hundred thousand billion dollars, if the price of gold could be kept stable.

The international monetary system was quite plainly in a somewhat delicate position. For one thing, the French President had insisted on converting the whole of France's dollar reserves into gold. Worse, he had persuaded the Germans to do the same. Essentially all of the reserves of the European Economic Community were in gold. Frankly, if the bottom were to drop out of the price of gold, Europe was in the soup. No good European then–least of all the French President–could contemplate a fall in the price of element 79. Nor were the Americans anxious to think of Fort Knox as an esoteric junk yard. Russia too had mining interests, as had a dozen other articulate nations.

The British were smart enough not to put very much gold

onto the market. Just enough was released to balance the chronically adverse trade balance. So the price was kept stable through restriction, as the price of diamonds had been kept stable for a generation or more. The Chancellor on Budget Day was now able to hold up his battered old box with a real smile, not the ghastly gray smirk of former years.

Yet the government was not without conscience. The story of the buried "talent" in the Bible came repeatedly to their collective mind. It was felt that the enormous golden windfall should somehow be put to progressive use. Modernization, automation, this was the obvious direction in which Britain should go. Plainly, the gold should be used to finance such a development. Snag, the trade unions, the lotus-eaters.

Automation, it had to be admitted, would put a lot of people out of work. But wasn't this just what the unions themselves had really been seeking, these many years past, to have their members working as little as possible? What the unions obviously wanted for their members was to be out of work but not out of a job. The solution to this apparent paradox came in a brilliant flash to an administrative genius in the Civil Service. Unions should be paid for *not* working. Whenever automation made work unnecessary, payment would be made to the appropriate union, exactly as if its members were still doing the work. So it came about that the concept of "automation money" became of decisive importance in the evolution of British society.

"Automation money" was thought of as a perk in the beginning. Soon it became a right. Everybody wanted it. An insistent clamor arose for more and more automation. Unions became overwhelmingly powerful. Since automation money was paid through unions to members, there was no hope at all for you unless you had a ticket. Without a ticket you had to work, just the opposite from the way it used to be. Union membership soon increased to the point where union-sponsored parliamentary candidates were always elected, and where it was really mere hairsplitting to attempt to distinguish between the unions and the government.

The system works smoothly, the economy purrs along. Britain has become the most automatized nation on Earth. New technology is now bought from poorer nations, nations like the United States, where the unfortunate people are still obliged to work. Nowadays, the British take things easily, in well-bred style. Nothing reflects the national temperament quite so much as cricket. No game of cricket ever finishes nowadays. Gone utterly are the ferocious drives and swings of former years, gone are the chops and hooks. Perhaps twice in an hour a batsman will permit himself a gentle tickle to fine leg. The huge crowd wakens up for a brief moment to give a round of restrained applause, for here at last is the nirvana foreseen so percipiently by the philosophers of the East.

THE JUDGMENT OF APHRODITE

Hermes gave the contenders a quick, experienced glance. A weird lot, a distinctly unpleasant lot, was his instant analysis. He was damned glad he wasn't going to find himself frolicking with any of 'em. He doubted whether Aphrodite quite realized just what it was she was letting herself in for this time.

On the far left was a fellow in a yellow cape, a king of some sort. Every fifteen seconds or so he spat a stream of bright red liquid into a huge spittoon. He squirted it out, blood, presumably, from the side of his mouth in what he evidently thought to be a stylish fashion. Thus relieved, he looked around the room with a satisfied smirk. Then he would chew for a few seconds and out would come the next jet.

The one at left-center needed close watching. For a moment

it would be a handsome young man, not much different from Hermes himself. Then, in a flash, it would be a long, drawn-out old man banging away at the floor with a heavy cloven hoof. Another flash, and it would be a toothless hag in a battered hat who sat there leering up into the face of the blood-spitting king. A trick cyclist, if Hermes ever saw one.

At right-center sat a patriarch with a huge white beard, fully a yard wide. He sat motionless and quite without expression.

At extreme right, equally motionless and equally expressionless, was a thing. Essentially all body, broad with a thick chest, it had a face of a sort, the features apparently of gilt. Hermes had the fancy the features consisted merely of gilt lettering, but this seemed absurd.

Aphrodite floated in to the sound of exquisitely delicate music. Simply but superbly dressed, she took her accustomed chair on the raised dais. Hermes caught a glimpse of the fabulous legs and sighed.

The king in the yellow cape was the first one up. "I am Tamerlenk, conqueror of nations, conqueror of mankind." A veritable torrent of blood swished into the spittoon.

"I see a beautiful country before me, a land golden with ripening corn." The fellow threw out his cloak, as if to suggest yellowing fields. Then he pointed straight ahead. "*I* will have that country. I will have every last thing in it, every woman, every man, every child. With subtle potions I instruct my soldiery to intense greed and cruelty. I inflame them to intense lust. I drive them like the whirlwind into the land of the ripening corn. Women are raped before the eyes of lovers and husbands, men are flogged until not a piece of flesh will cling to the bare bones. Terror reigns supreme, terror untempered by pity. Then I hold up my hand–so!–and peace descends instantly on the land. All is now silent and still, and with silence comes abject obedience from every man, every woman, every child. The land is now *mine,* every last thing in it.

"This is no vainglorious boasting. The pages of history stand open to attest to my conquests. I waste no more words. Power lies in strength, not in words, and the true servants of power are the whip, the chain, and the branding iron."

Tamerlenk gave a last decisive ping into the spittoon and sat himself down, plainly satisfied with his performance. Well he might be, thought Hermes. Aphrodite was making notes in her special little book, the way she always did when she was impressed. This monster had hit Aphrodite's weakness—the exercise of brute physical force—slap-bang on the nose, just as Ares, the war god, always seemed able to do. Hermes had a sudden suspicion of this Tamerlenk fellow. This might be a trick by Ares himself, a trick to maneuver himself into bed with Aphrodite. Once there, once home again, as it were, it wouldn't be hard for him to make her forget their last quarrel.

Why must it always be the screwballs who were attractive to women, the plausible rascals and the pathological idiots? Hermes shook his handsome young head, and sighed again.

The trick cyclist was the next one up. In the guise of the old crone in the hat, the creature began in a high falsetto. "I frighten the maidens of the villagery. Sometimes I skim milk, sometimes I labor in the quern, and bootless make the breathless housewife churn. Sometimes I make the drink to bear no barm. Sometimes I mislead night wanderers. Hee-hee! Laugh I at their harm."

In a flash the old crone was gone, replaced by a skull inside which a brisk fire was burning. The skull itself seemed to be inlaid with turquoise mosaics. Before Hermes could make quite sure of this, a creature with lank, black hair parted down the middle, a creature with a vast mouth—the teeth even and flat at the bottom like a pair of scissors—was standing there. This apparition immediately gave way to an oddity with the horns of a cow, the teeth filed into sharp needles this time. The gyrations went faster and faster until Hermes became quite dizzy. Aphrodite turned on him with a quizzical shrug.

"I haven't the slightest idea how the idiot got himself in here," he muttered apologetically.

Aphrodite had seen enough. "Stop it!" she snapped. The

command was not to be ignored. The gyrations halted dead. It was the thin creature standing there, the one with the cloven hoof. Hermes noticed it had a big black tail, a tail which twitched continuously. The thing seemed incapable of being still, even from one second to the next.

"I am the Devil," it began.

"Never mind who you are. What's all this twinkling in aid of?"

"Those are the many guises of my assistant devils. I have many assistant devils, at my orgies."

"What orgies are these? Will you be good enough to *stop twitching.*"

The Devil swiveled uncomfortably on his cloven hoof. His case wasn't going any too well. The thrashing tail was stilled for a moment. He must think up something to show off his power. "I have an enormous orgy starting promptly at midnight on Walpurgis night."

Apart from the merest whistle through the teeth, Aphrodite took this absurdity with complete composure. "Will you be good enough to define the word 'orgy?' Exactly what goes on in an orgy?"

"Well, devilry, of course, generalized devilry. I get 'em all going round and round in a wild dance, faster and faster I force 'em to go. Until the first cockcrow."

The Devil started up quite a realistic drum roll with his hoof. Aphrodite and Hermes exchanged glances. Neither could remotely conceive of why the first cockcrow should have anything to do with it.

"I instructed you a moment ago to be more explicit. *Who* are *'em*?"

"Damned souls, of course, out of graves gaping wide. I open up the graves of all damned souls on the nights of my special orgies."

"*What* is the purpose of this ridiculous nonsense?"

"Everlasting torment, my dear lady. Hell is my kingdom. In hell everlasting tortures are inflicted on the hosts of the damned. Following this little session, it is my intention to enjoy an extended interview with the damned soul who immediately preceded me. I'll soon have him spitting out of the other side of his face, I promise you."

The Devil beat out a veritable tattoo with his tail. Hermes had the feeling the creature could give you a really nasty thwack with that big black tail. He also had the feeling Aphrodite wasn't going to put up with this nonsense for very much longer. Her voice was already dangerously silky. "How would I go about it, becoming a damned soul?"

"Nothing easier," said the creature cheerfully, "particularly for a woman. Just get yourself seduced."

"Really, as easy as that?"

"Nothing more needed, one of my oldest tricks. Just get yourself solidly seduced."

Too late, the Devil realized his foolish mistake, talking nonsense about seduction to the very goddess of love. He started his twinkling tricks again, hoping, no doubt, to confuse the issue. Hermes could see the skull with the turquoise inlay, then the scissor teeth, then the cow horns, round and round in a whirling kaleidoscopic display. Aphrodite gave the big thumbs-down, and like a flash Hermes stabbed the button. In the merest fraction of a nonosecond, the ground opened up at left-center.

The Devil was gone now, but the noise he was still able to kick up with his drumming hoof rumbled up from the depths below, more than loud enough to be a nuisance.

"Better clear him altogether," muttered Aphrodite.

Nothing loath, Hermes pressed the clear-store button. Instantly the noise stopped, but in its place a vast sulfurous cloud of smoke belched up out of the floor like some enormous geyser. Hermes just managed to punch the air-conditioner before the smoke entirely blotted out the console keyboard.

The incident did not improve Aphrodite's already shortening temper. The acrid smoke left her with red-rimmed eyes, not at all becoming to any girl. Hermes could see things were going to be a bit tough on the two remaining contenders. Yet neither showed any sign of apprehension or even of inconvenience. Up came the fellow with the enormous beard. Hermes would have predicted the fellow would be equipped with a massive voice, it just had to be so. Sure enough, the Voice boomed out, "I am that I am." Nothing more.

"I am that I am," repeated Aphrodite. "What d'you make of that one?"

"Shortest possible logical closed loop," answered Hermes. "Just two interlinked transfer instructions."

The fellow continued, "I am the god of Abraham, the god of Isaac, and the god of Jacob."

Aphrodite's rippling laugh echoed through the hall. "Who are Jacob, Isaac, and Abraham?" Answer there was none. The bearded patriarch stared dead ahead, his eyes focused on infinity. Hermes pressed the query button. It took a second or two for the search to be made. Out came the information on the high-speed printer.

"Nomads. Complex sexual situation. Small-time stuff," he said.

"Rather what I expected. This fellow has delusions of grandeur."

Aphrodite was on the very point of a thumbs-down when the Voice intoned, "I live on a throne, high and uplifted. Above it stand the seraphim."

Hermes watched as Aphrodite's wonderful mouth opened wider and wider. In astonishment, she asked, "*What* are seraphim?"

"Each seraph hath six wings. With twain they cover my face, with twain my feet, with twain they do fly."

Once more the laugh with all sunlight in it rippled through the hall. This time the patriarch heard it. With an expansive smile and a guffaw he boomed, "One day I called Samuel, and Samuel rose up and said, 'Lord thou callest me, I am here.' So I said unto him, 'No, Samuel, I called thee not, lie thyself down again,' whereupon he laid himself down again."

Aphrodite smiled in her silkiest style. "Let me remind you, I am here to make judgment on a reasoned case, not to listen to drab anecdotes or feverish pronouncements. Suppose you apply yourself to a little coherent thought."

The fellow stood blinking for quite a while. At last some recollection crossed his mind. "I visited Sarah as I had spoken, and did unto her as I had spoken."

"What had you spoken?"

"That Sarah shall bear a son. That Abraham's seed shall prosper."

"I asked you a moment ago to make an attempt at rationality. How could Abraham's seed prosper if it was *you* who visited Sarah? What were these unmentionable things you did to her? Did you give her a little pleasure, a little kindness? Or did you treat her with the summary dispatch of a farmyard animal?"

Ignoring these pertinent questions, the patriarch lifted his right hand high above his head. "I am a jealous god," he thundered, "I have smitten the first-born in the land. I have caused the waters to close upon mine enemies. I have made the ground to tremble beneath their feet."

To emphasize his point, the patriarch began to blow out through pursed lips in the manner of a horse. At first there came nothing but a woofing, exactly in the manner of a horse. Then ever so slightly the ground did indeed begin to tremble. Fascinated at this discovery, the fellow went on and on with his woofing. More and more he got the trick of it, until quite suddenly there came a really violent shaking. A glass of fruit juice at Aphrodite's elbow jiggled and spilled over into her lap. The liquid instantly soaked its way through the resplendent dress. In a fury she shouted, "Stop this ridiculous and childish nonsense!"

There was no stopping it. The Voice boomed on. "I am the lord of hosts. In the beginning I created the heavens and the earth. My spirit moved on the waters."

The voice of Aphrodite, as she rose from her chair, was also loud and threatening. "Quiet, or I will have you cleared, utterly and finally, so that not a single absurdity is left behind."

Heedless, the Voice ranted on. "Come then, gather unto my supper that ye may eat the flesh of kings, the flesh of captains, the flesh of mighty men, the flesh of horses, the flesh of all men both great and small."

Hermes glanced again at the data sheets from the printer.

"Raving lunatic. Worst case of paranoia on record," he shouted.

At swelling volume, the creature continued to give tongue. "Come, look here," it thundered, "look and ye shall see. I have a name written on my thigh–king of kings, lord of lords."

"This one's got the lot," bellowed Hermes in Aphrodite's ear.

"Then give him the lot," she bellowed in reply.

Hermes extended a deliberate finger to the oblivion button. Instantly, Whitebeard was gone, the ranting stopped. But not without all trace. Like the Devil, this creature vanished in a pall of smoke, this time a sickly smoke–incense, apparently–worse, if anything, than the Devil smoke. Hermes was too taken aback by the intensity of it to reach for the air-conditioner. Yet the pall gradually cleared, and with its clearing Hermes found Aphrodite clinging to him.

"I suspected something like that might happen," she whispered, "I got to the controls just in time."

Aphrodite resumed her judgment seat with as much dignity as she could muster, It wasn't easy to be dignified, for the tumbler of spilled juice had made her abominably sticky. Never again, never again, she decided, was she getting herself into a situation like this. Even the blood-spitting Tamerlenk was fast losing his attractions. Aphrodite was just on the point of making a reluctant judgment in favor of Tamerlenk when a discreet cough reminded her of the fourth contender. The thing was standing there, a big rectangular box with a shining gilt face. It had legs, after all, extremely short, stumpy legs. The face really was nothing but gilt lettering. The thing began in a flat, featureless voice. "In a very real sense, I have been gravely perturbed at the manner in which business has been conducted today. I am referring now, not to the summary dispatch of the two immediately preceding gentlemen, but to an omission on the part of the Chair to state our terms of reference. An observer, *persona curiae,* might well be pardoned for failure to comprehend what this affair is about. I will commence, therefore, by stating terms of reference from the floor.

"Power is the subject of our debate. The contenders, each one of us, has appeared here freely, without constraint or duress. It is the opinion, the belief, the conviction of each one of us that power over the destiny of man resides chiefly in our person. It is my belief that power resides in me. Each of the gentlemen who preceded me held a similar belief. We are here to provide evidence to substantiate our belief. It is the task of the Chair to weigh our several arguments and then to deliver a balanced and final judgment (I might add, parenthetically, that the Chair has graciously condescended to spend a night of extreme frolicsomeness with the winner). These are our terms of reference."

Hermes saw the dark look on Aphrodite's face. No objection, he knew, would be made to an immediate punching of the windbag button. Yet in all fairness, a thumbs-down could hardly be given on anything the gilt creature had said so far. Besides, Hermes had no wish to leave the field open to the blood-spitting merchant. The flat voice continued. "The contention which I am here to prove is that *I,* a book of rules, a *mere* rule-book, if you prefer to call me so, exercise complete sway over the destiny of man. From front to back, top to bottom, I am a vast aggregation of laws and statutes. With these I bind my subjects far more effectively than the fetters employed by the remaining gentleman on my right. The gentleman imagines himself to be a conqueror. Yet where are his conquests? Are they not all gone now, like thistledown blown away in the wind? *My* conquests become more firmly established as time goes on. My rules become hallowed by time. My laws become established by precedent. Learned men search me from cover to cover, lavishing their energies and talents to insure that I am obeyed in all things, down to the last comma. Strong men quail before me quite as abjectly as they ever quailed before the gentleman whose spittoon is now very definitely spilling over onto the floor of this otherwise clean and pleasant hall.

"As the centuries pass, I hold dominion over an ever-increasing proportion of humanity. Throughout the so-called advanced countries, I control the lives of the people down to the finest details. In one of the oldest of these countries, I have reduced the people to an ultimate paralysis, a paralysis in which no decisions can be taken, a paralysis in which nothing happens except endless and futile argument, utterly without point or urgency. In this last stage, I reduce all humankind to an intellectual senility in which they even become incapable of responding to the most elementary facts.

"A remarkable aspect of my power is that my victims never regard themselves as victims. The more I reduce them to a state of complete inanition, the happier they become. Astonishingly, I do not even write my own laws or my own statutes. I allow humans to pack into my massive chest anything that should take their fancy. This explains why I am quite largely stuffed with rubbish. I contain outrageous logical contradictions. Far from hindering me, this even helps my purposes, for humans torture themselves over the contradictions, not by a genuine removal of logical difficulties, mark you, but by setting up elaborate pretenses that no such contradictions exist. These pretenses greatly assist me in inducing mental collapse in otherwise quite rational and healthy people. I cause mental agony on a vast scale, far more effectively and acutely than the whips, chains, and branding irons employed by the remaining gentleman on my right.

"Absurd talk, you might be disposed to think. Absurd, indeed, but true, utterly true. Why, you may wonder, do they not destroy me, these foolish humans, why not burn me, disintegrate me—eh? Here's the rub, they cannot do so. *I* cannot be eliminated, because no human organization can succeed without me. Particularly, no army can fight without me. An army without regulations is but a rabble. Now suppose some section of humankind sought to manage without me. It would have no army, save a mere rabble. It would be overwhelmed by the armies of those humankind who pay allegiance to us. It would be wiped from the face of the earth."

Hermes shifted uneasily. A dread of this gilt-faced creature was beginning to grow within him. There was a curious conviction in the flat, unemotional voice, so sharply in contrast to the other contenders. Aphrodite was feeling it, too. Her face was a chalky-white, for no doubt the thought of a night's frolic with this appalling thing was beginning to prey on her mind. The creature went relentlessly on. "Let me pass next to an exposure of the weaknesses in the arguments put forward by others who spoke before me. Throughout his former career, the gentleman of the many faces—whom you so rightly converted to a puff of sulfurous smoke—failed in everything he attempted. He failed precisely because he could never bring himself to accept the need for rules and regulations. Had the gentleman ever been able to organize himself, to draw up a rigid and extensive code of sinning, there is no telling to what heights he might have climbed. By nature, if I may be permitted the term, the gentleman was anti-everything, anti-rule, anti-law, which, by the way, is why he smelled so very badly in his final moments.

"The gentleman of the large beard and overpowering voice presents us with a more complex problem. You must understand, my dear young lady, that this gentleman in his time enjoyed a considerable vogue in the world. Many indeed will be distressed to discover him converted so adroitly to a whiff of incense. His passing will leave regrets."

The gilt rule-book paused for a moment, a dramatic pause. "Now what, we must ask ourselves, lay at the bottom of this vogue? The fact, no more no less, than that the gentleman in question employed my services from the beginning of his career. My services seemed attractive to the gentleman exactly because of my policy of allowing everyone to write his, or her, own laws and commandments. Permit me to read a specimen of the laws written by the bearded gentleman."

Fascinated, Hermes watched as the creature slipped a scroll of parchment out from its belly. Screwing up the gilt face, almost as if it were adjusting a pair of spectacles, the creature intoned in a weird singsong falsetto, "The woman who lieth carnally shall be scourged with rods. The man who lieth carnally shall make offering of a ram to the priest, for his sin is grievous."

The creature proceeded to pull sheaf after sheaf of scrolls from its chest and guts, tossing them with a contemptuous gesture high into the air.

"A wonderful relief, I might say, to be freed from all this ill-mannered rubbish. Still, it bears directly on my point. The former patriarchal gentleman made great play with his rules, regulations, laws, covenants, and commandments. It was just this mass of restrictive rules that gave him an uncanny influence over certain segments of humanity. Yet the power was mine, really. Behind the scenes it was I who manipulated the strings on which the gentleman and his followers used formerly to dance."

"Have you finished?" Aphrodite asked wearily.

The creature seemed to smirk. "I have reached the end of my case, a case so clear, so decisive, that your judgment, my dear young lady, is now but a trivial formality. However, before leaving the floor I wish to offer serious advice to you and to your friends.

"Ask yourselves why in the last score of centuries you have been so strangely in eclipse. The hirsute gentleman, the gentleman of the many faces–I take them together, for the two were really in conspiracy, a point which I imagine escaped you—exercised a greater influence than all your many exceedingly quick-witted friends have been able to do. Your most remarkable discoveries in the technological field have brought a measure of recovery in recent years, it is true, but the weakness remains. Unless the weakness be removed, I fear we shall have a relapse on our hands. The urgent need is to appreciate the need for *me,* the need for an enormous complex of restrictive rules and regulations—what you may eat, when you may eat it, what you may drink, when you may drink it, when you must breathe in, when you must breathe out, regulations and laws for everything. If the patient is to be fully restored to health, this is the way it must be. There must be none of the old free and easy habits."

So saying, the strange creature with the gilt face resumed its seat. Hermes drew in a deep breath. In his view, there couldn't be any doubt about it. By rights the creature had won. He didn't expect Aphrodite to see it that way, not when her eyes were so set on the Ares-like piece of pork. She'd leave him to dispose of the gilt windbag. By rights he ought to give the thing an honorable discharge. With something of a shock, Hermes realized, this wasn't at all what he'd really do—his finger was already itching to press the incendiary button. He'd burn up every last rule, every last regulation, every last little scrap of parchment, every last little particle of gilt.

Aphrodite stood. She made her announcement in a curiously flat voice. "My judgment is in favor of the gentleman on the right. To him I award the prize of a night's frolic." Turning to Hermes she added, "Return the gentleman on the left to his particular niche, wherever that should be."

Then she walked down the steps from the dais, gracefully in spite of the juice, to where the gilt creature was sitting. It rose and took her arm in a stumpy paw. The two of them moved slowly out from the Judgment Hall.

Hermes was left with the problem of the disposal of the spittoon character—a veritable river of blood was streaming now across the floor. The stuff had the appearance of welling up out of the spittoon, as if from an obscene spring. If this abomination was what he claimed to be, the solution was easy—simply to press the return button. But if this were not Tamerlenk, the situation could be distinctly awkward. Ares would quite certainly be bull-mad at losing Aphrodite.

If it really was Ares, sitting down there, Hermes knew he'd have to watch out for himself. Keeping a wary eye on the creature, he moved toward the console. A high-velocity jet screamed past his ear. The stuff splattered against the wall with the thunder of a vast waterfall. Hermes dodged as the next broadside burst like cannon fire from the gaping mouth of the war god. The game was to make him run for it, to make him run like the wind. Not for his life must he run, for in the way of things Hermes was immune from death, but to save himself from being knocked silly. His every instinct shouted for him to get out of this place, to flee before the furious rage of Ares himself. Hermes fought back his fears. He threw himself into cover behind the console. Searching the keyboard, his finger came down on the morpheus button, just as the console itself was hit.

There was a deep silence. Hermes struggled to his feet. The console was now a twisted mass of smoking metal. Ares lay supine on the floor of the hall. Hermes walked slowly to where the war god lay, weltering, it seemed, in a sea of blood. But Ares was not dead, Ares was in an endless sleep, a sleep from which the strongest injections of hate could never waken him. There would be no more rivers of blood, no more memories of war, no more memories of women raped and men flogged.

The first light was dawning when the gilt rule-book slipped out of bed. The creature was distinctly loath to leave at so early an hour, but it was utterly imperative to reach the draftsman without delay, before the world woke to a new day. In the heat of passion, a jug of juice had spilled over his gilt front, and a good deal of his ink had run, blotching and blurring more than one critical statute, more than one *nudum pactum.*

The rule-book glided away, thinking smugly to itself that Aphrodite was happy, satisfied, and sound asleep. Actually she was none of these things, quite the reverse. She was pretending to sleep in the hope this appalling bore would stop whispering his favorite ordinances in her ear. She was unhappy, frustrated by decisions postponed, decisions requiring further investigations and further probing, decisions referred back for consideration by alternative bodies.

The miracle happened and the thing at last quitted her boudoir. Aphrodite stretched herself in the hope of stretching away the feeling she'd got of being packed tight in cotton wool. Out of nowhere it seemed, she had an astonishing idea. In amazement she wondered why it hadn't occurred to her long ago. Reaching over, she grabbed the pink bedside telephone.

Hermes woke from restless sleep. Wearily, as he answered the call, he wondered what next. Then he heard Aphrodite's whispered invitation. In a flash, he was out of the bed and out of the window with the lightning speed given only to the messenger of the gods.

THE OPERATION

From his earliest years, young Joe was a bright lad. He was the best of his group at everything, a good worker if need be, but mostly he managed things so easily he hardly needed to work very seriously. He mixed with the other members of his group, appearing socially well-adjusted, until they were past puberty and were all reaching the right age for the operation. Then he began seeking after knowledge he wasn't supposed to have, particularly history, the history of long ago.

There was a girl at the crèche. He and Pat had grown up together. Joe had always like the girl, ever since they were tiny kids. Now, as they were growing older, he liked her a whole lot more. She let him kiss her, of course, she'd always done that. Joe was more than a bit mystified why things hadn't gone much further. It wasn't Pat who was stopping it. Nor could it be the grown-ups, Joe could run rings round the grown-ups. It could only mean the monitoring control was aware of Pat and him, and was arranging it so they could never get alone together in the right sort of place.

One day Joe did have a success, not with Pat. He managed to get himself locked overnight in the big library. During the long hours, he found a way into the room containing the forbidden books, the books which were still kept as a matter of record but which nobody, except some occasional old scholar, was permitted to read. He found most of the things he wanted to know. The picture which had formed so far only in a shadowy outline in his mind jumped now into sharp focus. With clarity came decision. A fierce determination swept through the boy. Come what may, he would not submit to the operation.

The date of the operation, scheduled for all Joe's group at the crèche, was still a little more than two months away. Each day seemed neither longer nor shorter than it had been before. Yet taken together, one day following another, the months melted away like butter in the sun. All arrangements were made, times settled, his was to be about halfway through the morning. The youngsters were told the things they might pack for their convenience, amusement, and occupation at the medical center, later, when they were recovering. They were even given special traveling cases in which to do the packing.

The matron came to Joe's room on the morning. She came with an injection "to make it easier for him." It would take about one hour before it would put him really "out." That would be roughly the time when he would come before the "surgeons," not human, of course, for no human could achieve the dexterity of those mechanical hands, working both with extreme precision and at lightning speed. There was much to be done in the fifteen or twenty minutes allotted to Joe and to each of his group.

Joe had said nothing of his intention, not even to Pat. He

would have liked to have persuaded Pat not to submit, too, but then there would have been serious trouble for her as well. If Pat had been as worried as he was, it would have been different, of course.

The strange thing to Joe was that none of his group, himself excepted, had any real worries. They all accepted the operation as completely natural. Long, careful conditioning in the crèche explained it. The only thing worrying the others was the pain, the few days of exquisite agony which inevitably followed the operation, the pain which no killer had entirely succeeded in suppressing.

The matron's attitude toward the injection was a part of the conditioning. She behaved in a pleasant manner, as if the injection were of no more consequence than swallowing a vitamin pill. Joe was known to be a "difficult case," but there had been nothing in his behavior to suggest he might balk at this last stage. From time to time, the matron had dealt with youngsters who had become difficult or even obstreperous. This had always been a few weeks beforehand, so there had been plenty of time to soothe away any doubts by appropriate additives to the youngster's food. Joe had known this. Why permit them to drug him into stupidity weeks ahead of the critical moment?

This *was* the critical moment. Brusquely, he instructed the matron to go to hell. She told him not to be a silly boy, so he repeated himself still more forcefully. The woman was now at a loss. Already that morning she had injected a score of other members of the group. She took a large capsule. All she need do was to press it against the boy's arm, almost anywhere, then touch the release button and one of the battery of fine needles would be sure to penetrate a sensitive spot.

Joe saw the matron's hand reaching toward him. In a frenzy, he gripped the wrist and twisted hard. The capsule came free and dropped to the floor. Then Joe did something he'd wanted to do for a year or more, he slapped the matron just as hard as he could. He would have liked to have gone on and on slapping her, but once was enough. This wasn't the time to lose control of himself, once would be quite sufficient. The woman was well-proportioned. She could have returned the blow. Instead she groveled to him, as a beaten dog will grovel.

The matron was distinctly good-looking, in her early thirties. The desire to assault her nearly overwhelmed the boy. Then he remembered she was quite burned out. In a flash the desire was gone, to be replaced by a deep sadness for the woman. He let her go and waited. He tried to sit, but all he could do was to sit a bit, then shuffle a bit, then look out of the window. After half an hour they came for him, two medical orderlies. They were strapping, bronzed fellows. There was no point at all in resisting them, nor had Joe planned to do so. Probably they had orders to bring him by restrained force if necessary. So he went along with them quietly and without comment. He was gambling that if he went placidly they wouldn't force an injection on him at this stage. He thought they'd now wish to interrogate him, and the injections they'd need for the interrogation wouldn't be the same as the one they needed for the operation.

Joe had also gambled on the direction in which the orderlies would take him, past a certain bush in the gardens surrounding the crèche. Earlier that morning, he'd stuck a good stout stick vertically in the ground, so it looked for all the world like a part of the bush itself. The young fellows didn't march him aggressively now they saw he was so calm, for they were not conditioned themselves to be aggressive, or swift-moving. No grown-up was conditioned to be aggressive, for that matter. When they came abreast of the right spot, Joe darted with the agility of the young to the bush and pulled up his stick. Before the first man had recovered from his intense surprise at the lightning change in Joe's disposition, the boy hit him hard across the kneecap. The second man he hit furiously across the shoulders. Then, like the wind he was running toward the vehicle the men had brought, the vehicle in which he planned to escape into the wild country.

There were lots of communities like the one Joe lived in scattered over the Earth, maybe a hundred of them. Nothing of a material kind ever passed between them, except sperms for breeding purposes. Uninterrupted electromagnetic communication passed between the different centers, but the content of that communication had nothing to do with humans. The only thing electromagnetic to do with humans was the light entering their eyes and, of course, the general monitoring itself. The nearest other community was something like three hundred miles away. Joe wasn't exactly sure, because there hadn't been anybody who could tell him. Such information wasn't thought useful in any way. Nor had he been able to find much on this topic during his nocturnal prowl through the big library. At any rate, he knew there was something like three hundred miles of wild country, country without roads, without tracks even, except where tracks had been made by wild animals. It was a country of mountains, lakes, and forest.

His first problem was the vehicle. Although he'd never driven one before, he knew every detail about how a vehicle should be driven. But knowing how to drive and actually driving are two different things, as Joe speedily discovered. Still, he did manage to get the machine working. He did manage to make it move in a crazy sort of way. The drivers of other vehicles saw something was wrong and quickly got themselves out of his path. It didn't take long to clear the few miles to the outer boundary of the community. Here he ditched the vehicle and set off into the woods.

Joe expected to be quickly pursued. They couldn't monitor him, of course, but they could order a general aerial search. He saw the more frenzied his flight the more obvious would his path be, and the more easily might they trace him from above. So he stayed quite close to the community. Once he had found good shelter, there was really little point in pushing on any further. Besides, the nearer he stayed to the community the better could he judge what actions were being taken. It soon turned out that no actions were being taken, for a reason Joe came quickly to appreciate.

In the books he'd always read that other animals were markedly inferior to man. Yet in their own world, Joe found this not to be so. His uninstructed efforts to trap and to fish met with negligible success. He found some edible fungi, clumps of wild berries, and this was about all. It was enough to keep him alive, but it was not encouraging for the future. The only aid Joe had managed to bring with him was a source of fire. Even this would become exhausted after a while. He saw he had badly misjudged the wild country. Only with risk now could things be retrieved. If he could find one, he'd simply have to try raiding an unoccupied Camp.

After a lot of weary slogging, he did manage to find a Camp that seemed to be unoccupied, but the buildings were solid, impenetrable to bare hands, even to sticks and stones. He was trying one of the smaller buildings when he was horrified to hear a voice behind him. "Ah, I thought you'd turn up sooner or later, young fellow-me-lad."

In panic and anger Joe swung round to find it was only an old man. Joe had seen him often enough in the community, but had never spoken to him.

"Hee-hee, gave you quite a start, didn't I? Suppose you take a look at this, eh!"

"This" was a basket, quite large, crammed with food. The starving boy grabbed it without comment and began to wolf its contents. He'd never eaten so fast in his life, or even conceived it was possible to eat so fast. Not until he was completely stuffed did the boy give any attention to the old man. Then he said, "How did you know I'd turn up?"

"Because I knew you'd be hungry. You see, I did the same myself once."

"You mean you refused the operation?"

"Yes, I did the same as you, made the same break into the country. But I had to come back in the end."

"So then, they made you have it?"

"No, they didn't."

Joe glanced quickly at the old man, but he couldn't tell anything, because the old fellow had a good-sized hat well pulled down. The train of thought must have been obvious, for the old man chuckled and said, "I'm not going to take it off, just to gratify your curiosity. You believe what I tell you. They didn't force me to have it."

"Then what did they do to you?"

"Nothing, nothing at all, and they'll do nothing to you. It's no good, you going off again into the country. There's no way there. The only way is for you to come back with me."

Joe thought he saw what the idea was. "So that's why they didn't bother coming after me. They got you to do it instead."

The old man looked a long time at the boy and then shook his head gravely. "Listen, my young friend, do you really think they, *they,* have need of *me* to do their work for them? D'you know what they'd have done if they'd really wanted to bring you back?"

"An air search."

"Nonsense, not with you unmonitored. You could hide for a million years out there. For a bright lad you show a surprising ignorance."

"So there's nothing they could do except send you."

"Don't you know there's a kind of animal with special gifts for tracking? You give it the smell of somebody. The clothes you left behind had your smell, my boy. Those animals would have followed wherever you went, through the woods, over the hills, down the valleys. When they came at last upon you they'd simply have held you there—until an aerial vehicle arrived."

Joe did remember reading something like this somewhere. He had a feeling the old man was exaggerating and he wondered why. The old fellow got up from a sitting posture and added, "Now I think it's time we stopped all this nonsense and started back home."

Naturally, Joe had no intention of going with the old man.

Saying he would think about it, he seized the remainder of the food and made off at a run into the forest.

During the next two days Joe did in fact do a lot of thinking. From his earliest years he'd been taught that it was quite impossible to live in the wild country. All the children in his crèche, all the children in every crèche, were impregnated with the dangers and horrors of the wild country. All his experience seemed to show this was right. Yet, was it really right, or was it just a clever illusion? The information about animals, about their simplicity, perhaps even that was part of the deception? Joe saw the beginnings of a plan now. It meant returning to the community. There was no help for it but to return, unfortunately, because he hadn't done his preparatory work properly. In fact, he hadn't done his preparatory work at all. Which was where he'd been deceived. Joe knew he'd have to go very slowly and with the utmost caution.

The matron received him back at the crèche as if nothing had happened. Nobody attempted to molest him, just as the old man had told him would be so. It meant *they* were playing a game, just as he himself was beginning to play a game.

In the next few weeks there was a good deal of spare time, because his group were still away convalescing. Joe read mostly the things he was supposed to read. The illicit things he did only in tiny fragments. He also walked about quite a bit. He'd become used to the feel of his legs while he'd been out in the wild country. It made him horribly restless now, being cooped up in the crèche.

One afternoon his wanderings took him to the thing he hated most. It was a building, massive and strong, entirely without windows. It was built in a circle about a mile in diameter. In the center he could see the cluster of high towers from which all the monitoring was done. There were two entrances, Joe knew, but only one could he see. The other was concealed from all but the special servants. Only they knew the manner of its opening. The entrance Joe could see was as plain as it could be, a wide-open entrance. It led nowhere, of course, except to the cubicles, the cubicles which every grown-up member of the community visited every two weeks. Joe watched people coming out and going in. They were paying their compulsory visits to the cubicles as if it was the most natural and normal thing to do.

This building, so forbidding to Joe, but taken so much for granted by the others around him, was the home–or rather, the housing–of *they*. People always referred to the thing as *they,* but how did anybody know it really wasn't *it?* Perhaps there was only one. Then there'd have to be just one of the things in each of the other communities. Perhaps somewhere there was a completely dominant *one,* perhaps even the thing in this building. Joe allowed himself to toy with the wonderful airy dream of destroying it, just as he'd done hundreds of times before. For years he'd lain in bed at night building fantasies around this idea. But now he saw it couldn't possibly work that way. Even if this one could be destroyed, there would still be all the others, hundreds of them. Even if he destroyed the dominant one, the others might again be able to make another dominant one, like bees can always make a new queen.

Joe turned over in his mind some of the forbidden things he'd read in the history books. The worst thing of all, really, was the incredible complacency, the incredible selfishness, of the generations which had brought this situation to pass. The foremost scientific authorities of bygone ages had solemnly declared that inorganic instruments could never be dangerous, because it would always be necessary for them to be programed by man. Idiots. Even while such statements were being made, the facts were already pointing in exactly the opposite direction. Surgeons, human surgeons, had already discovered simple forms of behavior which could be induced, whether the subject willed it or no, by electrical potentials imposed on the brain. This discovery had come during brain operations–with the brain exposed, the electrical fields could be imposed quite simply from outside. The next stage had been to insert electrodes in the brains of animals. Fierce animals could be rendered tame through such devices. Still nobody saw the obvious implication, even though electronics had reached the stage of micro-miniaturization. The implication which everybody, except imbeciles, perhaps, should have noticed was that the interior of the bony structure of the skull could be permanently impregnated with a complex mass of ultra-sensitive miniature electronics. With the skull replaced, there would be no need for crude electrodes sticking out from the head. Signals from outside could be rectified within the head to produce a highly configurated electric field. The principle was already there in the dim, distant reaches of history. Superlative technical skill was needed to convert the principle to a reality. The intervening centuries had supplied the skill, and now it was humankind itself that was being programed, exactly the opposite from what the wise men of history had asserted.

Joe looked across at the inner towers. It was from those towers that the monitoring signals issued, directing and controlling the brain of every "grown-up" in the community. By definition, a grown-up was simply someone who had experienced the operation. With the exception of Joe himself, all his group were grown-ups now.

One possibility would be to stop the signals going out from the towers. Yet even if there should be a natural interruption to the flow of signals, due to some unexpected defect, perhaps, Joe saw the grown-ups would be foolish enough to repair the defect. With the monitoring turned off, rivalries would soon develop, and out of those rivalries one group or other would carry through the repairs. Indeed, this was exactly the psychology of the way power had passed gradually to the inorganic instruments. Down the centuries, it turned out more and more that a group of humans could acquire power over other humans by itself yielding power to the inorganic instruments. The more you yielded yourself up to those instruments, the more you could impose your will on other humans. There was an inevitable natural selection in it. Paradoxically, ambition and the insistent desire to dominate contained within themselves the seeds of servitude.

The last step toward servitude came with the offer of immortality, or what seemed like immortality, to a number of renegades, whom Joe hated above all else. The thing in this grim, gray building was no longer purely inorganic. It had many actual human brains, or portions of brains, integrated into itself. This was why the controls were so delicate and why the special servants were needed. Joe had never been able to discover exactly what status the human brains occupied in the total functioning of the *thing*. His suspicion was that the brains were merely used as ancillary instruments, as "lower centers." Yet they enabled the thing to understand human psychology, to understand human psychology through and through. It was only after brains had become a part of the thing that the monitoring system itself was gradually developed.

The bitterest aspect of the monitoring was the relentless way in which steps were taken to insure the full efficiency of the control, by means of highly compact storage devices placed inside the skull of every grown-up. It was just in order to have these devices checked and read that all grown-ups were required to pay regular visits to the cubicles. Because of these visits, imposed by the monitoring control, it was impossible for grown-ups to plan subversion. It was impossible for them to escape in a geographical sense, as Joe had done. They were prisoners, emotional toys in the hands of a pitiless master.

The time came when Joe's group returned from convalescence. He'd expected to see far more in the way of ugly wheals on the upper part of the skull. It was only because the hair was still growing that the mark of the operation was at all obvious. It was easy to see why you had to look hard, once recovery was complete, to see the tiny telltale line in the hair growth. The operation produced essentially no departure from normal, so far as outward appearances were concerned. Even so, Joe had the feeling of something unclean about the whole lot of them. The strange thing was they all seemed to feel the same way about him. Only too obviously he was no longer their natural leader. They made him feel more and more the odd man out. Only Pat tried to treat him normally. She even wanted him to kiss her. There wasn't anything in the kisses, but Joe was surprised the monitoring control didn't stop it. The control could easily have made Pat freeze up completely. The situation must be completely known, because Pat was paying regular visits to the cubicles, just as all the other members of his group were.

The days slipped by. Joe played his hand very slowly, taking the steps he had to take one by one, often with a couple of weeks separating consecutive moves.

One morning, Joe came down to the usual communal breakfast to find the whole of his group gone. This was the day Joe had dreaded for so long, the day of the first Camp. He hadn't told Pat anything of the real purpose of the Camps. This was one of the things he'd learned in the big library. The principal object of the Camps was to shatter the sexual drive of all young grown-ups. Joe could see enough of the point of view of "the other side" to understand how much of a nuisance sexual drive would be if it pervaded the community. It would destroy the crèche system, which permitted such careful conditioning of the young. Love would induce rivalries that might soon destroy the carefully knit communal life. Sexual drive might even cause men and women to become brave, even to resist the dominance of the thing in the building without windows. Sexual drive might cause ordinary men and women to attack and destroy the special servants of the thing, whatever the cost to their reason and sanity. Joe could understand why sexual drive had to be rigorously controlled. What appalled him was the calculated way in which it was destroyed.

Since the operation on his group, it was obvious nothing of sex had passed through the minds of the group. Joe could tell this, because there had been nothing of the smutty little jokes which had been a part of their daily life before. The sex had been quite turned off by the monitoring control. He knew this too from Pat's kisses, they were the kisses of a little girl. The sex in his group had been canceled quite completely. Joe couldn't understand why this wasn't sufficient, why there was any real reason for the existence of the Camps. All he could think was, there might not be any reason, the *thing* might take a kind of pleasure in the Camps. Human brains were integrated into the thing. Joe more than suspected that human brains might be playing an important part in directing the control in this one activity, at least. Those brains, the brains of the renegades, might derive constant pleasure from this complete emotional dominance of their own kind.

What would happen to his group, once they were comfortably installed in the Camp, would be quite horrible. The Camp itself was a spacious prison from which escape was impossible once you were inside it. Everybody would be made to leave, the cooks, the drivers, maintenance men, everybody except his group. Signals would be made to radiate throughout the Camp. The signals, against which you were utterly defenseless once the operation was performed, would have the effect of sharply reversing the sexual inhibitions which had been imposed on the whole group over the past weeks. Everybody would think it tremendous fun the first day, even the first two or three days. But hardly on the fourth or fifth day, and certainly not by the tenth day. At that stage the whole group would be in a temporarily shattered condition.

In a group as young as Joe's, the return to normal would be fairly quick, perhaps two or three weeks. Memories of the first Camp would become distorted, in the sense of pleasure remembered and exhaustion forgotten. The group would even begin to look forward to its next Camp. This would take place after an interval of about two months. The same pattern would be repeated. It would be repeated again and again for a space of about five years.

At a certain stage, however, usually about eighteen, a general dread of the next Camp would begin to cloud the whole of a young person's mind. The dread would become stronger and stronger as one Camp followed the next. Yet still there would be no intermission, no mercy from the thing in the building without windows. In these last years, usually nineteen or twenty, it would be necessary for the signals in the Camp to become much stronger, to produce an equivalent response. In fact, over the whole five or six years the driving signals would be steadily increased. The process ended only when visits to the cubicles at last showed the individual's sexual responses to have been finally burned out. So at the age of twenty or so, the exact age differing a little with the individual, every grown-up in the community became quite sexless. The matron of Joe's crèche and the two bronzed medical orderlies had all been completely burned out, nothing of the normal responses was left.

Although the girls were as much affected as the boys, they were not in any way incapacitated so far as child-bearing was concerned. From twenty to twenty-five was the usual period for child-bearing. The children were artificially induced, and were sent at birth to one or other of the several crèches, where they would spend their entire lives until the time of the first Camp. Some few young men were required to deliver the sperms for the artificial induction. The young men were selected on the criteria of intelligence, submissiveness, and physique. Joe qualified on the first and last of these. An intense display of submissiveness in the months preceding the operation would almost certainly have singled him out as a breeder. He himself would have been given no choice, of course. This was exactly why Joe had made his stern decision. His refusal to submit made it certain that, even if the operation were forced on him, he would never be "awarded the status" of a breeder, he would never be obliged to father thousands of children into a life of helpless bondage.

Joe knew his group would be moved out of the crèche immediately following the first Camp. He wanted to see Pat once again, in spite of what must have happened to her at the Camp. He found her quite easily, almost as if she had been deliberately put in his way. Nor was it difficult for him to get her to himself for a while. When they were alone, out-of-doors, she looked at him with big, haunted eyes. He expected her to cry, as she had done when she was a little girl. Instinctively, he put his arm around her, just as he had done when they were both small. The mere effect of his touch was to produce intense shock. Poor Pat, his Pat, her face went utterly vacant. The mouth opened and slobbered. He laid her on the ground, patted her cheeks, and shouted her name. Within less than a minute she recovered, the vacancy was gone, and there was the same dumb look in the eyes. Joe took care not to touch her again, allowing her to get to her feet without help. He didn't know what to say, so he simply turned away, walking as fast as he could, his eyes blinded by tears.

Joe made his preparations quickly. He knew now what *they* were doing, he knew why they had let him come back. For weeks past, nobody had spoken to him properly, only the occasional monosyllable. He was utterly without friends, without anybody to consult, ostracized by his own human community. The one person he really cared for they were destroying quite deliberately under his very eyes.

There was just one thing more he wanted to know. Joe found the old man at last, the one who had brought him the food. The man was still wearing the same hat well pulled down. Joe asked him, "Why did you let them do it?"

"For the same reason you will, because there is no other life for you. Suicide or this, that's the only choice."

The man took off the hat and Joe could just barely see the division in the hair. "How did you go about getting them to do it? Nobody's been near me. You were right about that."

"Nobody will come near you, my boy. There'll be no offers to you. It's *you* who'll have to go and beg *them* now, young fellow-me-lad."

"Is that what you had to do?"

"That's what it came to in the end. Mind you, I stuck it out longer than you've done. But there's no other way. If you play your cards right, they'll take you back and forget the whole thing."

"How do I go about it?"

"Just tell the matron at your crèche. That'll be enough to start the ball rolling. They'll interrogate you a bit, and you'll have to go down on your knees a bit, of course, but it'll come out all right in the end."

Joe thanked the old fellow and said he'd think about it. Since their last talk he'd learned a lot more about animals. With animals called elephants, tame ones, he knew, were used to catch wild ones in the old days. He knew it really wasn't necessary to tell the matron, the old man would do all the necessary telling. It was so obvious. His case was being carefully documented. The idea was to make him into a tame elephant, to show younger wild ones what might happen to them if they too were to resist. It was to be an exercise in ultimate submission.

He went to see the matron and told her he was thinking of changing his mind. Instantly she became quite friendly and said he was making a wise decision. Joe said he would let her know finally within a week. Then he stole the last of the things he needed.

A vehicle was on its way out to one of the Camps. Inside was a chattering throng of youngsters of about his own age, not his group. He waved at them and they waved in return. He followed the vehicle for a couple of miles or so, as if he were only out on one of his usual walks. Then he cut away into the woods, as he had done before.

This time it would be quite different. This time he had the right sort of weapons, taken from museums, knives and simple firearms, sufficient to pick off any dogs they might send after him. There would be no more trying to fish with bare hands. This time he had hooks, and he knew how to make more hooks should he lose the ones he'd got.

Joe had done everything possible, read everything possible about the old lore. He must learn to survive, at first with the help of the tools he had brought with him, then gradually without them. This was his one and only problem, to survive. Everything else would follow. He would let it be known in the crèches that he had survived, all the young would know, in the years before the operation. The operation couldn't be performed much before fourteen, not while the skull was still growing. Up to fourteen the youngsters could still think for themselves if they wanted to do so. Because of the incessant conditioning, because of the breeding for submissiveness, there wouldn't be too many at first. But there would be some. If only in ones and twos, there would be some who would join him, sufficient for a little band to become firmly established.

Joe had now fully understood the inner weakness of the system he had to deal with. It was utterly efficient, utterly ruthless, in meeting any threat from within. It was very nearly helpless against any threat from outside. Appalling weapons could of course be made, but who should operate them? The thing in the grim, gray building was static, it must have its human servants. It must have submissive servants, not aggressive ones. How could submissive humans fight? Under attack the grown-ups would simply grovel, exactly as the matron of his crèche had groveled. Joe had no doubt that submission could be changed to aggression by the monitoring control. He had no doubt the monitoring control could reverse things, just as easily as it reversed things sexually. It would be possible to change every grown-up into a wild, ravaging, murderous monster. Weapons in the hand of such monsters would eventually be turned against the master, however—this was where the weakness, the instability, lay. It might not happen the first time, but it would happen sooner or later, so long as constant pressure from outside could be maintained.

Joe also understood why there were many communities on the Earth, all well separated from each other. Comparatively small communities were much easier to keep under rigorous control than a single very large community would be. Granted no rivalries between the *things* in the different communities, this was the logical way to do it. The big areas of wild country between the communities supplied natural protective belts. The wild country made it hard for the very young to escape. But Joe *had* escaped. Now he must survive. Then he must build his band, small at first, bigger as time went on. They would lay siege to the communities, destroy water supplies, capture the young, terrorize the old. Joe had once read of the sacking of an ancient city. The description of a palace running with blood, slippery to the foot, caught his imagination. If ever he and his men captured a community, then indeed the building without windows would be made to run with blood, the blood of the special servants, the blood supplying the biological components of the *thing*.

There was no point this time in staying within close reach of the community. Joe headed for the interior country, moving steadily and confidently. On the fourth day he crossed the first of the mountain ranges. In the valley below he could see woods beside a shining river. He made his way downhill with a lighter heart than he ever remembered, the boy who was the best intellect his community had produced in a dozen generations, the boy with the courage to turn his back on ten thousand years of progress. Like another boy in distant antiquity, condemned to the wilderness, robbed of his girl, he would return one day to be a scourge to the whole world.

ABOUT THE AUTHOR

Fred Hoyle, Plumian Professor of Astronomy and Experimental Philosophy at Cambridge University, has been a Fellow of St. John's College, Cambridge, a staff member of Mount Wilson and Palomar observatories, and Visiting Professor of Astronomy at the California Institute of Technology. His scientific studies include Frontiers of Astronomy *and* The Nature of the Universe *(the book that introduced the now famous steady state theory of creation). Among his works of science fiction are* The Black Cloud *and* Ossian's Ride.